Rise

Sequel to Stray

Nancy J. Hedin

A NineStar Press Publication

www.ninestarpress.com

Rise

© 2021 Nancy J. Hedin

Cover Art © 2021 Natasha Snow

Printed in the USA

ISBN:

First Edition, March, 2021

Also available in eBook, ISBN:

CONTENT WARNING:

This book contains depictions or mentions of a deceased relative, the death of a prominent character, homophobic slurs, transphobia, references to male rape, grief, Islamophobia, references to suicide, mental illness, mention of trauma, and assault (recounted).

Lorraine Tyler is finally at veterinarian school with her best friend and roommate, Frankie. She's also got a girlfriend who likes to play naked hide-and-seek.

Life in Bend is pretty great for Lorraine until she hears the voice of her dead sister Becky in her head, pointing out Lorraine's failures past and present.

Her problems don't end there. Her dad is hospitalized, leaving her heartsick at the thought of losing him, and there has been no justice for the hate crime perpetrated against Lorraine's friend Ricky the year before. As if those things weren't worry enough, Lorraine's former and present girlfriends are in town seeking her undivided attention. No wonder Lorraine's wacky therapist has her eating bean soup and counting up the traumas of her life.

Lorraine and Frankie juggle their own personal crises while they try to navigate family relations and work for a more just and LGBTQ friendly community for everyone who calls Bend home.

For Tracy, Sophia, and Emma and in memory of Mom, Dad, and David.

Chapter One

The Voice

It was the middle of the night and I wanted my momma. I don't think I've ever said those words as an adult, but I was really scared. The voice was back. It had abated during finals and I thought perhaps my sister had stopped haunting me. No such luck. Becky had been stubborn and relentless in her life. I suppose it should have been no surprise that she was the same in death.

My twin sister Becky had died the spring before we both would have turned nineteen. Until recently, when I made twenty years old, I had only been plagued by the memories of her violent death. During the end of my first summer session of vet school something new had started happening. I was hearing Becky's voice and a running commentary on what I should have done to save her life and what I was presently doing to mess up my life. I had two weeks off from school to get this latest disaster managed.

I could but wasn't allowed to call Momma. It was too late at night. She said phone calls in the middle of the night should only contain extraordinary news like a birth or death. Even car trouble was not a permitted excuse to call home after 10:00 p.m. or before 6:00 a.m. Momma said, "Call AAA. Don't call our farm." I watched the clock as Becky yammered in my head.

"Lorraine, you're on a brief summer break starting today, but don't think you don't have to study. Wouldn't it be ironic if after all this time waiting for the right moment to leave home and the money to go to vet school you flunk out?" Becky cackled at her joke.

"I'm not going to flunk out," I said into the room and regretted it immediately. My roommate Frankie roused from her drunken sleep.

"What? What's going on?" Frankie raised her head and looked in my direction. Her five-o'clock shadow was already showing even though she had given herself a very close shave before going out the night before. She was in the early stages of transitioning male to female—living her truth. For Frankie that meant coming out to friends and family, hair removal, and saving, saving, saving. If Frankie chose to pursue the surgical route the expenses were astronomical. Frankie joked she would be at the craps table in Vegas rolling the dice and shouting, "Come on, Momma needs a vagina and new pair of breasts."

"I'm sorry, Frankie. I was talking to Becky."

"Her again? God, the dead are chatty." She put her head down and then lifted it again and said, "Did I tell you? I heard voices yesterday. They said, 'Freak, faggot, failure!' Oh, wait that wasn't psychotic voices. That was my father talking to me." She put the pillow back over her head to sleep.

Frankie had been disowned by her family, but her father still called every single day. I'd heard Frankie's side of that conversation for months. To me it seemed like every call and every periodic visit devolved into harsh words and blaming, not from Frankie. She always kept her cool and reminded her parents that she loved them and always would.

I sympathized with Frankie but had my own critic to manage. Becky spoke up again,

"Frankie will never, surgery or no surgery, be as beautiful as I was my senior year. Let's talk about me some more, Lorraine. You know what's funny? I can remember the feel of the gasoline on my skin, the sting of it, its odor in my nose; and I can recall the force of the knife as it entered my surprisingly flat belly, but I can't for the life of me remember the feel of the fire."

I bolted into the bathroom and vomited in the toilet. No, I didn't find it humorous or oddly interesting that she couldn't remember the feel of the fire on her skin. I couldn't forget the image; the smell of her burning hair and flesh. Those odors were tendrils that wrapped around the little hairs in my nose and kept the sensory experience always at the ready to accompany the soundtrack of Becky's screams. I didn't say anything to her about the screams I heard. I didn't want to make her memory worse. I just wanted her to shut up.

"You know, Lorraine, if you'd been quicker and more planful you could have saved me. I suppose you were preoccupied with your own queer drama as usual." Her voice was matter-of-fact, but every syllable condemned me just the same. She was right of course. During the time of her illness, I was licking my wounds because I'd lost the scholarship, and there was never enough time for me and Charity. I wasn't thinking about Becky every minute when I should have been. It wasn't that I hadn't already told myself the same thing—every day, every hour, but to hear her say it felt like more of an indictment and final verdict.

I slammed the bathroom door. No matter, she was in my head, not the bedroom area of the apartment I shared with Frankie.

Becky sighed loudly, "Now, Little Man is growing up without his mother. I know Kenny got married again. He probably had to do that. He wouldn't have gone without sex for very long. Still, it should be noted that sociologists have concluded it's best for a child to be with his mother."

Mentioning Little Man, Becky's son and my nephew, only made me feel worse. I wanted to argue the point, but I couldn't.

I was of the opinion that it wasn't so great that Becky and I were with our momma? It wasn't for me. That was certain. But our situation was different than Little Man's. He wasn't a twin. He needn't compete for limited resources or audition for the favored position like Becky and I did.

"Back to my original question. You're the medical expert. Why didn't I feel the fire?" Becky persisted.

My phone read 6:02 a.m. Finally, I could call Momma. I called the landline first, hoping she was there at the kitchen table of our farmhouse pestering Dad with some complaint or request, but still feeding him a heart attack breakfast. I pictured her rising, the legs of her chair scraping against the tired linoleum floor, her bunny slipper clad, size nine feet padding across the kitchen, and her reaching for the yellow wall phone by the cereal cabinet and just above Dad's junk drawer. Dad was closer, but Momma knew he hated the phone and wouldn't answer it unless he had to.

No answer.

I pictured my dad readying himself for a day working at the lumber yard. Had he drunk his first or second cup of coffee? Had he snuck to the barn for his first filterless Camel cigarette? Had he slumped forward with his usual and now more frequent coughing jag? Had he spit into his red or blue bandana handkerchief?

Maybe he fended off Momma's criticism with one of his blessed animal stories. They were blessed unless you were the one who had to do the research at the library and figure out the lesson to be learned from screwworm 1960 or big breasted chickens or bonobos. It wasn't really so bad. I loved reading about animals. I just didn't like hearing I had so much to learn about how to treat people. I suppose my dad is one of the reasons I love animals so much. He taught me so much from his animal stories.

Back in the living room Frankie stirred and mumbled something in her sleep. I called Momma's cell. It went straight to voice mail, which was a torture in and of itself. Her cheerful voice followed by obvious information that she hadn't taken the call, an Old Testament Bible verse about the Godly and ungodly—I knew where I'd been sorted in that scenario—and a command to leave a message. I didn't leave a message. What was I supposed to say? "Hi, Momma, should I be worried that your dead, perfect daughter Becky is a voice in the head of your living and always disappointing queer daughter, me?" I didn't leave a message. I'd call someone else.

I almost called Twitch next. Twitch is my friend, mentor, my dad's best friend, and recently I'd found out he was Becky's and my biological father. Momma had a brief encounter with Twitch when she first came to town, before she met and fell in love with my dad. Becky and I were Benjamin Twitchell's blood, but Joseph Tyler's children. I clicked off the phone.

"Screw it, I'm driving to Bend."

Becky sneered, "Lorraine, you finally got away from Bend and what do you do? You go right back there. You seem destined to repeat all your mistakes."

"Shut up."

Frankie roused again. "What, was I snoring?"

"No, go back to sleep. I'm going home for a while." Besides, the last time I talked with Marin England she had promised me a game of hide-and-seek at her house. That was a PG-13 euphemism for her hiding naked in her king-size bed and me finding her before the covers settled. Yep, I was going home to Bend.

I stuffed some clothes and toiletries in a duffel bag, grabbed my phone charger and a couple of textbooks. Just before I made it out of the door I glanced at the tumble of limbs, hair, and blankets that was Frankie. We'd planned to do something with the big empty wall in our living room during break.

Becky said, "You might as well bring Frankie along. She'll fit right in. Pay attention, Lorraine, you might learn something from her."

I nudged Frankie's shoulder. "Frankie, Frankie, I'm going home to Bend. Do you want to come with me?"

Frankie launched out of bed, hurled razors, chemical hair remover, curling iron, beauty products, and her loosest-fitting clothes into a gym bag, a blanket and pillow in another duffel, and charged to the door.

For some reason Frankie liked visiting Bend. Don't get me wrong, I love Bend and planned to have a vet business and live there for the rest of my life. Still, it surprised me when others who hadn't grown up there found an emotional connection with the place. She said she could be herself in Bend. She didn't mind the looks or questions. I'd warned her I knew a gay man who had been beaten in Bend. I'd introduced Frankie to my good friend Ricky and his lover Russ.

Frankie stopped packing and searched for her phone. "I better call Mom and Dad and tell them I'm going. The cell reception in Bend is for shit. I don't want them calling me to tell me how disappointed they are in me and not being able to reach me. They'll worry I'm in a clinic somewhere losing my Johnson."

"You don't have to babysit me when I do this. I know you're tired from the first summer session." I touched her arm.

"Of course, I don't, cis, but I want to do this. Maybe I can be of help or at least amusement." She found her phone, kissed my cheek, and launched her bag of clothes at me. "I better pee." She exited to the bathroom and closed the door.

"God, you smell like margaritas," I called after her.

"Did I mention I'm learning Spanish?"

"Spanish? Right. Does that just mean you drank all night at a Mexican restaurant and flirted?" I didn't say it, but I worried she teased men who possibly would have beat her for being herself. I thought of my friend Ricky and what had happened to him along a field not far from our farm.

Frankie stuck her head out from the bathroom and talked around her toothbrush, "No, it was a meeting of LGBTQIA for civil rights. It just happened to be at an authentic Mexican restaurant with fabulous enchiladas and very spicy men."

Frankie joined every configuration of queer or transitioning group she could find, whether it was local or national. She attended meetings in person when she could manage, and scads of online meetings and internet chatrooms to organize protests and get out the vote efforts. Mostly she pasted and posted encouragement to others. As far as I could tell, community mobilization involved a lot of meetings that seemed more like raucous parties. Despite her many invites I had not joined any of the groups. I felt like my sexuality was a private thing. I didn't want to be legislated but I also didn't see myself as the poster child for any particular cause.

I heard Frankie's conversation with her parents from the bathroom.

"Yep, tell Dad that I still have my willie. I know you worry. I'll be with Lorraine in Bend. I just didn't want you to worry if you called and didn't get me right away. No, I'm not sleeping with Lorraine. I'm glad you'd be okay with that but it's not going to happen. Love you both. Goodbye." Frankie came out of the bathroom.

I grinned.

"You heard all that?" Frankie said.

"Yes. Do your parents really think we're sleeping together?" I asked.

"That was my mom. Dad was at the gym. I'm sure he'll be calling me before we make it out of town. Mom's so desperate that I keep all my nuts and bolts she'd pair me up with you." Her face turned sour before she kissed me on the cheek again.

Chapter Two

The Drive

I tossed both our bags into the truck bed, opened the driver's door, and waited for Frankie to get in and scoot across to the passenger side. Momma had hit the passenger side door of my truck when she was backing up her monstrous station wagon in the yard. I had bungeed the door closed and it was easier for passengers to enter from the driver's side. Frankie teased that I just liked seeing her beautiful ass as she slid across the seat.

Of course, Momma hitting my truck was an accident. Momma had routinely flattened lawn ornaments, outdoor grills, play equipment, and several lawnmowers. She refused to back down and couldn't back up a car worth shit. At least I wasn't in the truck at the time. Dad has an identical dent on his truck and reoccurring pain in his left elbow.

Before Frankie was cocooned with her blanket and pillow against the passenger door her phone rang. The ringtone was the Darth Vader theme from *Star Wars*, so

I knew it was her father calling. She stuffed her makeup bag on the floor of the truck, rolled her eyes, and took the call.

"Hello, Colonel." Frankie's father had been an army man. I never knew his actual rank at retirement because Frankie persisted in calling him different ranks depending on her mood. "Yes sir, we are about to deploy to Bend, Minnesota." She peppered her conversation with military jargon and no particular loyalty to any branch of service.

"Yes, sir, I have it with me in my pants and plan to have it when I arrive in Bend at approximately oh eight hundred. I will keep said weapon and have it here for your inspection in a few days." She looked at her phone and then smiled at me. "Apparently, he wasn't calling for an inspection of my schlong when he asked if I'd still have one when I returned home. I'll have to remember that when I want him off the phone faster. I suppose it gets him all worried that I'm suggesting he's gay when I confront his interest in my pecker."

"I don't know, but I suspect most men are cock-centric and would have a difficult time imagining losing theirs."

"Yeah, believe me, I get it. My choosing to transition makes him lock his knees together and cover his dick with goalie mitts. My being a woman kicks the shit out of the dreams they had for me." She looked at the big lake as she talked. "As mad as you get at your momma for not accepting you, don't forget, Lorraine. You took away some of their dreams."

I got it, of course; I got it. I just didn't know how Frankie could be so understanding and forgiving of her dad when he got mean and called her names.

"When my mom finally got pregnant the doctors told her she probably only had one chance at a viable pregnancy because of fibroid tumors," Frankie explained. "I was it. I was born intersex. I had what they called 'ambiguous genitalia.' My parents chose to make me be male. I don't think there's a culture in the world that would fault them for their decision. Males are top dogs. Here I am telling them they were wrong and not only that, I will put myself through drugs and surgeries to change it. I kicked the shit out of their dreams."

She didn't say any more. I suppose it exhausted her more than I could ever understand. She was asleep before we left Duluth city limits.

The truck radio didn't work. The tape deck was still mangling k.d. lang's *Hymns of the 49th Parallel*. I had no music to listen to. Against my will, I tuned in to Becky FM/AM.

"I'm sitting between you. I don't want any of Frankie's weirdness rubbing off on you," Becky squawked. "Next thing you know, you'll want a penis."

"It's not about genitals, Becky. I don't want a penis," I said louder than I had intended.

"What penis?" Frankie glanced from side to side like a gray squirrel.

"Never mind. I was talking to Becky. Go back to sleep."

Frankie snuggled into her nest again.

Becky whispered like she was trying not to wake Frankie. "Be sure to visit Little Man. Hold him for me."

"As if I'd ever go home to Bend without seeing him. Remember, we call Little Man Allan now. Kenny and his new wife Ramona insist on it. Allan's getting used to the change. He's three next month." That was a dumb thing to say. Of course, Becky knew when Allan's birthday was. I went a different direction. "Dad is head over heels in love with your son, Becky."

The cab of the truck was quiet for a few moments until the hamsters in the cage of my mind started running the wheel. As I got closer to Bend, signs sprouted from the fields and ditches promoting Warren McGerber for state congress:

Boots on the ground to protect the American family.

The admonition was like an apocalyptic scarecrow for me. I hoped it had a similar effect on voters. God, I didn't want him in a position of power or making policy for anyone.

"Frankie, look at all those signs."

She raised her head and peered out of the windows with squinted eyes. "Tell me again, what's a Warren McGerber?"

There were so many sarcastic ways to answer the question: Warren McGerber was a noxious weed, a scentless poisonous gas, a viper, but no metaphor was more telling than the plain truth of it.

"Warren McGerber is the brother of J.C. McGerber, a man at our church in Bend. It was J.C. McGerber who endowed a college scholarship fund in Bend. The scholarship was supposed to be awarded to the graduating senior with the highest grades. He gave it and then took it back from Becky first and then he took it back from me. That was rotten. I hated him for a long time, but he came around to do some good things. His brother, on the other hand, is evil. I suspected Warren McGerber was directly involved with beating and later trying to murder Ricky."

"Yes, yes of course I know Ricky. Ricky is yummy. So is that hunky hulk of a boyfriend of his."

"You think Russ is hunky?" Talking about the men Frankie found attractive reminded me a little of when Becky was alive and lusting after her future husband, Kenny Hollister. Although, I found Frankie less annoying.

"Don't you think he's handsome in that lumberjack I'm-going-to-carry-you-in-the-woods sort of way? It's a shame he's gay."

"Now Frankie, haven't you been telling me that it is important to accept everyone for who they are?"

She slugged me in the arm. Frankie bolted upright and grabbed the rearview mirror.

"Russ is handsome, but Ricky is beautiful. He has barely the hint of thyroid cartilage." Frankie massaged her Adam's apple as she peered at herself in the mirror. "Why didn't I have his hair and bone structure?"

I supposed Frankie's questioning and exploration of her gender identity and her desire to be her authentic self gave her license to bring most every conversation back to her body and worries. Gender identity is a pretty big deal in the world.

Frankie had taught me that I basically knew nothing about what it was like to be a trans person. Lucky for me, Frankie didn't give up on me as a friend. She had good reason. In those early days as new roommates, I put my foot in my mouth so often I'd chewed all the way up to my knee. We both knew something about being an outsider, but we didn't have the same life experiences and journeys. Frankie was my best friend and I believed she called me the same. Neither of us were able to process our lives with our parents.

She put her feet up onto the dashboard of the truck. "Look at my feet. How will any man love me with these big feet?" Frankie stared at her feet. I readjusted the mirror. "I'm thinking about cutting them off just ahead of that bumpy bone. I could wear those socks that have individual compartments for toes. They would give the illusion of toes."

"Will they also give the illusion of balance and being able to walk too?" I asked. "Your feet are fine. Lots of women have big feet. Having child-size feet doesn't make a woman. I just wouldn't suggest messing with your cuneiform bone." I didn't know why I bothered trying to impress Frankie with any anatomy or physiology I'd learned. She was a better student than me, even with all her worries about not having the body that fit her heart and soul.

"Another thing, you know what they say about the size of your feet and the size of your..." She wiggled her eyebrows.

"Yeah, big feet suggest a really big ego."

Frankie burst into tears and pounded the heels of her hands against the dashboard where her feet had been.

"What? What's the matter? I was joking about your big ego. I know you meant your penis." I examined her face wondering if I should pull my truck to the shoulder of the road.

"It's not that. Don't mind me. It's just that time of the month." She blew her nose on a T-shirt she found on the seat of the truck. My T-shirt.

"I support you, Frankie, but that's impossible," I said. The moment the words were out of my mouth I knew I messed up.

Frankie cut me a look. "Every day is that time of the month for me."

"I mean, it's impossible because women who live together get a synchronized cycle. We live together, but I don't have my period now, so I doubt you do."

"Nice try, Lorraine," Frankie said. "I don't need you to remind me that my body doesn't ovulate."

"Good grief," Becky chirped inside my head.

"I'm sorry I didn't say the right thing."

"I was trying to make a statement about my feelings." Frankie cried even harder, but she touched my arm. "You're so sweet. I'm crying because I don't think I will ever find love. You lesbians have it easy. You always find someone to nest with, even the lesbians built like refrigerators. If I have to save money for breasts, they should have to save money to buy a waist." Her bantering dried up as she sobbed, stuttered, and hiccupped. "I can save all that money, have the hormone treatments and surgery so that my outside matches my insides, but it doesn't guarantee anyone will ever love me."

No one's guaranteed that and no one is guaranteed that love will last. That's what I wanted to tell her. I didn't say that but something equally useless. "I love you." The assurances of platonic love or even familial love is ineffective in soothing the wounds of those who fear there will never be someone who will be head over heels in love with them.

Frankie wiped her tears and sat upright. "I'm not going to give myself over to maudlin preoccupation. If love is my destiny, it will come. I have those worries every so often like the hiccups and then they are gone." She composed herself again as quickly as she had collapsed. "Tell me about this McGerber creep."

"Okay. As I was saying, I'm certain it was his hatred for queers that brought Warren McGerber after Ricky and then me. Now he's attempting to bring his biases to state government. He's running on a platform of hate and angling to represent our district in state legislature. I've got to figure out a way to stop him from winning the election. He represents the Traditional Party."

"I like parties," Frankie joked. "Lighten up, Lorraine. If he's as hateful as you say, nobody will be dumb enough to vote for him."

"You know, there are people who will vote for a man like McGerber not because they are bad or stupid," I said. "They are loyal, patriotic, and often very generous, kind, intelligent people who will vote against their self-interests if they believe doing so will support their country or obey the tenets of their faith."

"Don't I know it. That's why I joined Democrats Against Meanies. DAM exposes hate-filled candidates who will gladly let someone else sacrifice their young men and women as soldiers, their money as taxes, and all their freedoms in order to keep the same people in power and riches. You couldn't have a Hitler Germany without ordinary people who just did what they were told."

"I don't know about all your groups, but I know I plan to do something to stop Warren McGerber from becoming the state senator representing our district."

"You are a very busy woman, Lorraine Tyler. It makes me tired just listening to the things you need to do on your own to fix this world. If I were Marin..."

Oh crap. I hadn't called Marin to let her know I was coming home.

Frankie continued, "If I were Marin, I'd be asking how far down the list I was."

"We're only a few miles from Bend. Do you want me to stop for you to do your makeup?" Frankie and I had an understanding that on all road trips I would provide ample stops for beauty and convenience food snacks.

Frankie rummaged through her makeup bag and began shaving with great concentration, which was probably wise since we were in a moving vehicle. She left me to my thoughts of Warren McGerber, Becky in my head, and now my neglected girlfriend. Great. I didn't tell Frankie about the promise of hide-and-seek.

Chapter Three

Welcome to Bend

Frankie was a hopeless romantic. If she had her way every person would focus on their romantic entanglements more than anything else. She was dying for romantic entanglements like most people. I understood the premise. It wasn't that my hormones no longer raged. I had my own entanglements, but other crusades seemed to march to the forefront compared to worrying about my dating relationship with Marin England.

What did I want? What did I value? I wanted my vet degree, and I was in school, but ideally, I wanted justice for Ricky. Justice meant holding Warren McGerber accountable for what he did. What he did to Ricky personally, and what he got others to do to Ricky and me when he was trying to cover up his hate crime. It wasn't that I thought every mistake a person made in their life should be revealed and held against them if they ran for office or became famous. People make mistakes and hopefully they change and grow. I did think it was important to look at the patterns of a person's life if they are being considered for a position of leadership. Nothing I'd heard suggested that Warren McGerber had repented for his pattern of hatred for queers, people of color, or anyone else different from him.

Ricky's beating was another horror film in my head. The only witnesses who could corroborate my suspicious were Ricky, who had lost his memory of the beating, two farmhands, Lewis and Petey, who had conveniently left town during the investigation, and Dr. Jacks, who was conveniently dead from sepsis in a wound I gave him when I shot him with my dad's double barrel shotgun. That was another story and picture I didn't need in my head, but at least he didn't talk to me.

When I reached Bend, Becky piped up, "Let's go to the farm first."

"I'm driving."

"Only because I'm dead," Becky pointed out. Leave it to her to remind me Momma had taken away my driving privileges back in high school because I'd brought a raccoon in the house. She had lifted the injunction when it served her purpose, like when she made me drive her and my dad home after Becky and Kenny's wedding dance. I had planned on Charity driving me home and receiving my first kiss from a woman. But no, that night Momma let me—no, insisted—I drive them instead. Of course, now I was grown, lived on my own, and had my own truck.

As I drove into town, I passed Twitch's lumber yard where Dad worked as inventory manager. He calculated the materials needed for various building projects and kept the floor inventory stocked. It was supposed to be less taxing on his body with better pay than the shingling and construction jobs he'd been doing. Dad's truck was in the parking lot. The beat-up Chevy made me smile. We weren't wealthy, but damn if we weren't rich. I didn't see my brother-in-law Kenny's truck in the lot but thought nothing of it. Kenny's whereabouts never interested me.

I drove by the Bend medical clinic where Momma worked. I didn't want to tell her about the voices while she was at the clinic, but it didn't matter. Her station wagon wasn't there. Strange. It wasn't yet nine o'clock. No matter, I made a U-turn by the barber shop. I could gas up the truck and drive to the farm. No doubt Frankie was hungry. Besides, I was in no hurry to talk about the voices I was hearing anyway.

*

I pulled into the new Munch and Pump for gas. Once she was within reach of convenience store snack food—she particularly liked the cheddar dogs roasted on rotating rollers under a plexiglass dome—Frankie crawled over me and out of the truck before I could dislodge myself from the driver's side.

"Do you want anything?" She called over her shoulder as she adjusted her skirt, brushing out the wrinkles from the summery floral fabric. I couldn't see myself in something so bright, but Frankie looked stunning.

"I'll come in when I'm done." I called back. "Then we'll drive to the farm." *Oh God, I wonder what Momma will say to Frankie this time.* Frankie had been to Bend a number of times before, but I'd shielded her from Momma's scrutiny as best I could. I could tell Momma wanted to barrage her with Bible verses about eunuchs and personal, impertinent questions. Occasionally Momma had outmaneuvered me and grilled Frankie about her "current parts and future configuration."

While I pumped the gas and thought about Momma tangling with Frankie, I didn't notice the tall man in a western suit who had exited the store. He stood over me.

"Miss Tyler."

Shit, it was Warren McGerber. How had I not heard his rattle and hiss before he was right next to me? I startled and nearly yanked the gas nozzle out of the fuel hole. I might have splashed him with a good dose of unleaded. Then, say a fella threw a match. I bet he'd feel it. Of course, I wouldn't do any such thing.

Regretfully, I was frozen in place. I let the creep talk at me instead of getting away from him as soon as possible. I figured he was too gutless to try to physically harm me in daylight, in public, but my heart clattered inside my chest. Instead, he implemented another tactic used by controlling, dangerous tyrants. He talked. His words battered and reminded me of what his hands were capable of doing. He didn't need to touch me. The potential beating was evident.

He looked around him. Maybe checking for witnesses. "I suppose that thing inside is with you. Another freak." He laughed.

Frankie. I pulled the nozzle from the fuel hole and replaced it on the gas pump. "Frankie is my friend. Just like Ricky is my friend. Neither one of them are freaks." I tried to sound calm, but I was shaking inside.

"Your friends"—he leaned closer—"nothing a good beating and being strung up to a fence wouldn't dissuade. I'd like to spend some time with this new one. Ask Ricky if his asshole thrums when he thinks of me."

Oh God, I thought I'd throw up or pass out. He admitted it. Just within my hearing. No one would believe me. He'd deny it. I would never tell Ricky what he said to me. Warren was a monster.

"Well, I must be off, things to do, people to see, and campaign money to raise. You see, Lorraine, I have many friends. More than you. I'm going to be a senator. Men can do great things with political power. I can't wait."

Frankie called me from the doorway of the store. "Get a move on, Lorraine. My sausage is getting cold."

Warren McGerber chuckled and walked away.

Shaken, I entered the store, paid for the gas, and scanned the store for Frankie like she was my child who had wandered away and could be missing or hurt. I found her in the chip aisle talking animatedly to a beautiful man I'd never seen before. He was darker than Ricky, taller than Russ, and muscled like a man who didn't buy his food from a place like Munch and Pump.

"Frankie? Have you got everything you need?" I called to her.

"Almost." She wasn't facing me, but I could easily imagine the smirk on her lips and the come-hither-and-come-again look in her eyes. I didn't plan to tell her what McGerber had said. I wanted to get away from the store and the air he'd breathed. Even Becky kept her trap shut. Maybe she was okay with what Warren had said.

Frankie piled her snacks on the counter, and I paid for them. The man held the door for her when she exited the store. I followed behind with the bag of food. He tried unsuccessfully to open the truck door for Frankie.

Asserting my existence that he had completely ignored, I said, "That door doesn't open any more since my momma locked it with the bumper of our station wagon. Frankie will have to get in on my side."

"Frankie," he said, treating me like I was scenery or elevator music. "What a wonderful name."

"Yep, she's Frankie and I'm Lorraine Tyler. This is my hometown. Just who are you?" I supposed I sounded rude, but I thought it was prudent to learn his name before Frankie ate him.

"I'm Justin. I attend the college in St. Wendell but I'm in Bend for the day or two visiting my friends, Ricky and Russ."

"You know Ricky and Russ? They're our friends too. Frankie and I will be seeing them later." He didn't look in my direction at all.

"Well, that means I'll be seeing you too. I'm staying with them a couple days or maybe longer." He answered my questions but stared at Frankie. He smiled a big grin of white, straight teeth. "See ya." He got in a Honda hybrid and drove away.

"All right, wipe the drool from your chin and get in the truck. Your sausage is getting cold."

Frankie got in and talked continuously as she filled her face. I missed most of what she said. Some of what she ate landed on the truck seat and dash. I didn't care. "Did you see him, Lorraine?"

"Yep, he's a big boy. He's hard to miss."

"Did you get a look at his feet? Do you know what I'm saying?"

"I know what you're saying, and I'd rather not think about it." I was thinking about Warren McGerber. He was so sure of himself that he could say those things to me with impunity. Maybe he knew there were always people in power prepared to protect men like him.

*

When we got to the farm, Momma's car wasn't there. I parked next to what had once been a small kettle grill until Momma had flattened it with her station wagon. The dogs ran to me with their tails wagging. They didn't jump on me. They just checked in before they crowded Frankie. After all, Frankie had been eating greasy sausages.

"Frankie, you remember Pants, Sniff, and Satan?"

"Yeah, what are you going to call the next one? Shit or Piss?"

"Don't be crass. Obviously, the next dog will be named Hump My Leg."

Frankie let the dogs lick her fingers. She rubbed their bellies and told them all about having met her future husband, Justin.

I called Momma's cell phone and got voice mail again. I called Twitch. Twitch picked up on the second ring. "State your name and business."

"It's me, Lorraine. I can't reach Momma. Do you know where she is?"

"I suppose she's at the hospital. I was just changing clothes to head over there again myself."

"Why's she at the hospital? Is she doing shifts there now too?" My momma was a nurse at Bend's medical clinic.

"No, she's with your dad. Lorraine, I'd have thought you'd be there too." There was a long pause on the line before he spoke again. "Shit. She said she'd take care of calling you. Shit."

"What happened?" I asked.

"Stay calm."

Those were useless words and anyone using them before breaking bad news should be slapped.

"What happened, Twitch?"

"This morning Joseph collapsed at work at the lumber yard. I took him to the hospital. They're saying he may have suffered a stroke."

"Oh, God. How can he have a stroke? He's not even fifty yet."

"I'll be sure to tell his arteries," Twitch cracked. "Could be genetics. Lots of conditions are even when you do your best to avoid them. He's stable. They gave him tPA to break up the clot."

I knew what tPA was. Dad had taught me about tissue plasminogen activators. It's a clot-dissolving medicine. They tested it on rabbits. Dad said it gave new meaning to luck you get from a rabbit's foot. I supposed that's true unless you're the rabbit.

"Can he talk? Can he move?" I panicked. I couldn't catch my breath. I grabbed the table edge to steady myself.

"I don't know. It's early." Twitch spoke calmly but he knew better than to bullshit me. "Do you want me to come get you? I'll do that."

"I'm not at school. I'm in Bend. I need to see Dad." I hung up the phone. "Frankie, Dad had a stroke. We have to drive to Langston Hospital."

"Shit." Frankie got back in the truck, sat upright briefly, but stayed quiet.

Becky on the other hand would not shut up. "Oh God, what if he dies?"

"Shut up, Becky."

Frankie looked over at me and rolled her eyes. She knew Becky and I were conversing.

"Worse yet, what if Dad doesn't die but he can't move? He won't be able to do any of his despicable hobbies like hunting, fishing, putting atrocious lawn ornaments in the yard, building bird houses or work at the lumber yard. Momma will harangue him, dress him like a doll, and run everything her own way."

"She runs everything already," I said treating the voice of Becky more as company than the pain in the ass it was. "But you're right. If Dad can't be himself, he won't want to be at all. You know what he'd miss most, Becky? Playing with Little Man."

Why hadn't I asked Twitch more questions? Was there a bleed? Did Dad break anything when he fell? Dad always said that if you break a hip and must go to a nursing home, you're a goner.

Dad was older than Momma, but he wasn't yet fifty. It seemed like he was awfully young for a stroke. Granted, I knew that lots of health issues were tied to genetics, and I didn't know much about Dad's. Like she knew my every thought, Becky said, "Do you suppose his people are still in Montana? I wonder what they're like?"

Dad's parents and brothers had left Bend for Montana when Dad was just a teen. He had remained in Bend, too stubborn to leave the land. He quit school, and except for a brief stint in the army he had worked two jobs and bought the family farm on a contract for deed. Once he'd paid enough of it down and had work history, he became an American dreamer entitled to the albatross of a mortgage. He gladly paid the bank every month to have his own land, house, and a few outbuildings. To my knowledge, he hadn't been to Montana and his family had not been back in Bend.

I sometimes told myself stories of what they might have done that made them leave Bend and never return. What were they like? Why had Dad never gone after them? Had I ever asked Dad about it? I wasn't sure. It was surprising Momma hadn't announced something about them especially if it elevated her. Then again, parents were a sore subject with Momma for most of her adult life. Her dad was dead, and she had only recently reunited with her mom who lived in a memory care home hours away.

I'd thought about losing my parents like most people naturally do. Usually, the thought was a pointed retaliation against Momma for something she'd done to me. I'd let myself fantasize about Momma conscripted to serve in a medical corps in someplace like Bangladesh. That was more wishful thinking than any serious contemplation of their dying. I think I had refused to imagine them gone. They had always been there for me. They didn't always approve of me, but they were there.

A new highway shortened the drive to Langston. What used to take nearly two hours was reduced to just more than an hour by cutting through prime farmland. That day I was grateful for eminent domain because it got me to Langston faster. I needed to see my dad.

Despite the shortened trip Frankie had again cocooned in her blanket and slept leaning against the passenger door. When I reached the hospital, Frankie remained asleep. Her pillow was drool sodden and she twitched and mewed occasionally like her dreams were good. Maybe she dreamed of Justin already. Maybe in her dreams she had her accessories and was enjoying how pretty she felt with Justin. I parked the truck and killed the engine. I remembered that she'd only been home a couple of hours before our trip. She had been out late celebrating end of term and learning Spanish. I got out of the truck, gently closing my door.

*

Once I entered the hospital lobby my nephew Allan came running to me and hugged my legs. My heart ached as I lifted him into my arms and hugged him. He was big for his age and talked a blue streak. Tears dripped down my cheek.

I'd helped take care of him after Becky died. He was my earliest understanding of what it meant to love a child, how it was different than romantic love or friendship. I'd kill to keep him safe and his every injury marked my heart as if the organ was now outside my body, somewhere on my sleeve.

I smelled his neck and hair. I detected bubble bath and maple syrup.

"Raine, Raine, Grandpa fell by paint and ladders."

"Twitch told me. Is your dad here?"

"Yeah, he supposes he hast to sit with that ornery Grandma until you get your ass home." The mimic didn't yet know that his impeccable ability to quote his dad would likely get his dad kicked.

"I'm here now. Aren't you going to daycare today?" I wondered why they didn't just let Allan go to the sitter.

Then it occurred to me they were probably worried Dad would die and they wanted him to see Allan.

"Dad's dropping me off and Momma Ramona is picking me up after."

Momma Ramona. I thought those words would have gotten Becky yapping again but she stayed quiet. Maybe she just looked at Allan through my eyes and vicariously held her sweet boy. I kept him in my arms a while longer.

"It's about time you got here." Kenny loped over to me like the stud he seemed to think he was. I'd grown to feel some affection for my brother-in-law. He took Allan from my arms.

"Now that's what I call a yummy man," Becky said. "Hug him, Lorraine. Kiss him for me."

My affections didn't extend to hugging and kissing Kenny. I preferred chewing him out. "I would have gotten here sooner if somebody had called me and told me what happened." I punched his arm but not nearly as hard as I wanted to. That public display would have to hold Becky.

Allan wriggled out of his arms and ran to the pneumatic doors in the entry of the hospital.

"Marin, you came. Charity, you came. Raine's here too." Allan took the hands of both women and led them toward me.

"Don't just stand there. Pick him up again. I need more time with him," Becky said.

Good grief! My dead sister was giving me orders in my head and both my former girlfriend Charity and my current girlfriend Marin were at the hospital. The prospect of talking with any of them at the same time made finding a chair by Momma attractive.

Allan, as young as he was, knew what to do. He hugged them both and then stood by his dad and sucked his thumb. Kenny smirked at me. "I'll leave you three to talk or whatever." He nodded at the women and took Allan outside to the truck.

What is the protocol here? Allan hugged them both in the order in which they arrived. Then he put his thumb in his mouth and didn't say another word. I envied his game plan. I hugged Marin first like he did. "Marin, thank you for coming. It's good to see you. Frankie's asleep in my truck. She'll be glad to see you too. She already met a love interest at the gas station."

Marin kissed my neck and grasped my hand. She smelled like spring and felt warm and curvy in my arms. My eyes drifted to Charity whom I could see over Marin's shoulder. I squeezed Marin's hand and pulled loose as I greeted Charity.

Was it my imagination or did Charity's eyes get big when she saw Marin kiss my neck and take my hand? I hadn't seen Charity since before she left for Europe with her ex-girlfriend Kelly. They were both artists and taking a trip of a lifetime. A trip that punctuated if not necessitated the end of Charity's and my love affair.

I had broken up with Charity the last time we'd spoken, and I had finally gone off to vet school. Had I told Charity, or had she heard that I was dating Marin? Who was I kidding? I knew very well I hadn't told Charity about Marin. We hadn't talked or written each other—well, I'd written her dozens of letters and not mailed a one. I had thought it was enough that I'd told Charity I wasn't all right with her being with Kelly for two years abroad and possibly wanting me when she returned. Ergo, we were both moving on.

So how come my body seemed like it had barely moved an inch? How come my body felt like I needed to nail my feet to the floor to keep from running to kiss Charity?

As for Marin, beautiful, strong, kind Marin, we were dating, and she was luscious. I had made it clear my priority was finishing my vet training so I could set up my practice with Twitch in Bend, but that didn't keep us from getting to know each other inch by inch and story by story. I was letting her be sweet to me and reciprocating the sweetness. When we were together, I barely thought about anyone else. We weren't married. I didn't have an exact word for what we were.

"You're back early. I thought you were traveling Europe for two years." I hugged Charity and tried not to linger. She smelled like strawberries and summertime.

"Yeah, well, Kelly found an interesting young docent in Italy and decided to remain in Rome a few months. I came back to St. Paul early." Charity sucked on her lower lip.

Yikes. I knew there was more to that story, but perhaps this wasn't the moment to share it.

"Dad called me in St. Paul early this morning. I drove home right away. Who's Frankie?"

Charity had called Bend home. That surprised and tickled me. I wanted to hear more about her European trip and early departure but held off with my questions, still in shock from finding out Dad was in the hospital. It was just as strange seeing her back in Minnesota and only a few feet away from me.

"Has Dad been here yet?" Charity asked.

"I don't know. I just got here myself. Momma didn't call me." It was familiar complaining about Momma to Charity.

Charity rolled her eyes and shook her head. She knew Momma's controlling ways very well. "Who's Frankie?"

Marin stood close to me and put her hand out to Charity. "I'm Marin. You must be Charity. I've heard a lot about you." They shook hands briefly.

"This should be good," Becky said. "It's bad enough you like girls, but now you're lusting after two at a time."

I wanted to deny that I told things about Charity to Marin but that was a useless lie. Besides, it wasn't like there was some sort of gag order on our relationship. Marin took my hand again.

Charity stepped closer to Marin. "You have me at a disadvantage. I don't know much about you. I know you're the social worker who helped Ricky when he was beat up, but it appears the two of you have more of a personal relationship. Of course, I have been away in Europe."

Charity didn't smile. Her lips were slightly parted and pillowy. She kept her eyes on Marin.

Becky growled.

"Shut up," I blurted out.

Marin and Charity both looked at me.

"Sorry"—I clutched my gut—"my stomach growled. I must be hungry." *I must be both reckless and stupid to be caught in this situation.*

Marin squeezed my hand and pulled me closer until our shoulders bumped. She smiled at Charity. "Yes, Lorraine and I are together." She looked at me. "We're happy."

"Well, at least she finally moved away to vet school. If she moved because of you, that's great," Charity said.

If that was the jab I thought it was, I didn't wait to see if Marin had a counterpunch.

"Point for Charity," Becky said.

"Who's Frankie?" Charity asked.

As though the third time Charity asked about Frankie was a magical spell, she appeared.

"I'm Frankie. I know who you are." Frankie hugged Marin, released her, and looked at Charity. "And who are you? You are lovely."

Charity blushed. "I'm Charity, I'm Lorraine's...old friend."

"Old flame is more accurate. You are every bit as beautiful as I was led to believe. I would absolutely kill for your auburn hair and perfect skin."

I'm pretty sure Marin's face reddened at Frankie's fawning over Charity. I wasn't certain which emotion surfaced on Marin's skin—was it envy or anger?

"Thank you, Frankie," Charity said. "How do you know Lorraine?"

"Oh doll, Lorraine and I are partners in crime at vet school. We're classmates and roommates. I'd share her clothes if she had any I'd be caught dead wearing. We tell each other everything." Frankie squeezed me against her.

"Okay." I broke loose from Frankie, rubbed my hands together trying to think of what to say to them. I couldn't take the pressure. "I haven't even talked with Momma yet. If you all will excuse me, I need to find out more about my dad." Coward that I was I slinked away to where Momma sat with Twitch. When had I ever chosen to talk to Momma rather than Charity or Marin? Never. Frankie followed me, her sandals smacking against the lobby tiles, but veered off to the bathroom when Momma looked up from her chair in the waiting room.

Chapter Four

Please Turn Off All Electronic Devices and Unnecessary Feelings

Momma hoisted herself from the industrial lobby armchair and hugged me which was an unusual occurrence. She didn't say anything nasty to me about Frankie being with me which was also unusual. I worried Dad had died.

She released me from her embrace.

"Momma, how's Dad?"

The vinyl covered cushion of the waiting room chair exhaled when Momma sat down again. I sat in the chair beside her. Twitch winked at me but knew better than to speak. Momma expected to have the stage.

"Oh Lorraine, God is punishing me for all the mistakes of my life and any other life I may have lived."

It wasn't like Momma to ever acknowledge having made any mistakes and for her to expound on reincarnation seemed like further blasphemy. I suspected this was a conceit and she would eventually bring the attention back to her superiority.

I knew in Momma's mind it was usually my doings bringing judgment from God to me and our family. Just before she went off to nursing school, she had said she had more understanding of the infinite variety in God's creatures. Taking a page from Dad's well-worn book, she had exhorted me to read about bonobos at the library. Her conversion was only superficial and temporary. Soon she was back to her attempts to cure me, convert me, or to cull the herd when it came to queers.

I let her continue her self-flagellation knowing eventually she'd turn her scourge whip, her words, back at someone else.

"How can God take Joseph? Joseph is so kind. He never hurts anyone. He works hard."

Twitch sat quietly nodding his head to the cadence of Momma's voice. She was preaching to the choir. Twitch and I were largely Dad's biggest fans.

All the things Momma said were true; and I must admit it felt good to hear her list off the good things she recognized about Dad. How long could this last?

"He drinks more than he should," she continued.

Okay, now I more readily recognized Momma's accounting system.

"He sneaks his filterless Camel cigarettes in the barn and makes more birdhouses than necessary. Don't get me started on the circus he's made out of our yard."

"Momma, how is he?" I pressed.

She continued with her litany of Dad's most recent transgressions according to the book of Momma. "Of course, recently he goes to flag meetings and gave five hundred dollars of your college money for a political barn dance."

Frankie was back. "A barn dance? For real? I don't know what I'll wear."

I looked at Twitch as if he were the interpreter for Momma speak. First, he looked at Frankie. "There's no barn dance. It's a town hall meeting." Then, he looked at me. "Joseph didn't give away any of your college money. He and some other folks covered the cost to add a town hall meeting in Bend. He wants Warren McGerber to answer some questions directly in front of voters."

I was still stuck on the five-hundred-dollar figure. "Does he get a quarter beef with that too?"

"No," Twitch said.

"Half a pig?" I asked, astounded that Dad would pay five hundred dollars for anything let alone an additional political rally.

"No! There's no meat involved," Twitch said. He looked at me like I might be slow on the uptake. "The two campaigns had already had town halls in bigger towns, including here in Langston. Your dad thought it was sensible to have one in Bend. In order to do that, we needed to pony up some money for the expense of the thing. I think the PFLAG group he goes to helped set it up."

"That's another thing," Momma interrupted. "Why does he need to go to that group on a Wednesday? He knows very well that I have Wednesday evenings off. He did it to spite me. Throw it in my face that when I am off, he drives to Langston to worry with other parents about their children."

"Lorraine, your dad went to PFLAG." Frankie was giddy with excitement.

"It wasn't to spite you. He hoped you would go with him and meet some of the other parents who have kids like Lorraine and Marin and Charity and Ricky and Russ and Frankie." Twitch shook his head. "Good grief, you are going to be able to field a softball team if your numbers keep growing."

I didn't say anything. I was still in shock that Dad had spent so much money and he was attending a PFLAG meeting. I didn't tell Twitch my aspirations went far beyond a softball team. I was a shitty softball player anyway.

"Could one of you tell me how Dad is?" I said.

"That's just it. I don't know. They won't tell me anything or let me see him." She held her hands far apart like she was waiting for someone to throw her a ball or a baby.

"Well, that's not entirely accurate, Peggy." Twitch took a deep breath, but his face remained a bit flushed.

"They sound like an old married couple," Becky said.

Twitch turned to Momma. "The nurse said he's resting; and you saw him briefly before you were kicked out of the emergency room and you saw him again for a few minutes before you were booted out of his room on the intensive care unit." Twitch tried to look stern, but I recognized laughter in his eyes. He knew Momma.

"You were kicked out twice?" This seemed excessive even for Momma.

"Yes, can you imagine?" Momma's eyes were huge above her high cheekbones.

"I for one can picture it easily," Frankie said.

I, too, could imagine, but I'd rather have seen it for myself. "What did you do?"

Twitch spoke again. "What did she do? She bossed people around like she was running the joint. That's what she did."

"Why hasn't Momma slugged him yet?" Becky said.

"I'm a nurse. I had some questions and concerns." Momma crossed her arms over her bountiful chest.

Momma had blazed through a two-year nursing degree and was nursing supervisor at the medical clinic in Bend. "It must be hard to not be doing everything you can for Dad yourself." I offered this crumb and meant it. "I suppose there's rules about it. You're a civilian when it comes to this hospital treating you or our family." Momma was used to being the officer in charge.

Momma stared at me, probably suspicious of my understanding, but before her gaze burned a hole in me, she turned to Charity and Marin who sat side by side directly across the aisle of the waiting room chairs from us. She glanced at me again, jerked her head in their direction, and said with more shout than whisper, "What are they doing here?"

"Momma, don't be rude," I said. Becky cackled. "They came out of kindness."

Momma sighted in on Frankie. She gave Frankie a full body scan.

Frankie didn't wilt. She posed. She lifted her head high, looked into Momma's eyes, and defied Momma to comment on her body.

"You're going to have a hell of a time finding women's shoes for your big feet," Momma said.

"That's why I'm here," Frankie said. "I was hoping you'd loan me some of your flats and heels."

Before Momma could respond, or possibly strike Frankie, I interjected, "They all care about Dad and they care about me. They're here to be of help and support." I knew Momma understood the concept but for some reason she questioned the idea when it involved queers.

Marin leaned forward with a manila folder in her hand. "Mrs. Tyler, I brought some paperwork along to get Joseph signed up for state insurance. I can help him, or you can fill them out."

Momma scrutinized Marin as if she might be trying to swindle our family out of the millions we didn't have and looked at the papers like they might be dipped in dung. Momma didn't touch them.

"Momma, you remember Marin. She helped us get insurance for Ricky when he got hurt." I offered this information in hopes the reminder would soften Momma. Momma adored Ricky. She called him the daughter she never had. Momma wasn't softened. She looked like she might bite Marin. I suppose contextually this would have been a good time to also assert to Momma that Marin was my girlfriend and I expected Momma's courtesy. I didn't say any more.

Momma nodded. "You"—she motioned toward Charity—"we've been praying for your safe travel in Europe. Aren't you supposed to still be there?"

"I just got back last week," Charity said. "Dad called me this morning when he heard about Mr. Tyler. He knew I'd want to be here for Lorraine."

That was probably the longest sentence Charity had ever spoken to Momma since we first got together. Her bravado with everyone else had never extended to my momma. I noticed she didn't extend any of her limbs toward Momma. I admired Charity's sense of self-preservation. Momma was like a tornado—just stay out of the way.

Momma glared at Frankie again but before she said anything, a nurse came out of the secured area and approached our clutch. She spoke first to Momma. "Mrs. Tyler, Dr. Jonas said you can come up to the floor to see your husband now." She looked at me. "Are you the daughter?"

"Yes." We all had our roles like a high school play. Momma was the wife, I was the daughter, Twitch was the good friend of the family, and Dad was the patient. I bet he hated being the patient almost as much as Momma hated just being the wife and not the hospital czar.

"I'm the wacky neighbor." Frankie stood up and took the nurse's hand. Then Frankie nodded toward Charity and Marin. "These two beauties are Lorraine's love interests."

I got the nurse's attention. "Please ignore my friend Frankie. She had ambiguous genitalia and now she has an unfiltered brain."

Frankie slugged me in the arm.

"You and Mrs. Tyler can both come up to Mr. Tyler's room for a few minutes." The nurse smiled rather sweetly at Twitch. "I'm sorry, Ben. You'll need to wait until family has had their turn. I could come back to get you when it's time." She mostly kept her eyes on Twitch. She ignored Marin and Charity and gave Frankie a double take.

I caught Twitch's eye. "You'll have to wait, Ben." I rolled my eyes.

He reddened but didn't speak.

Momma cleared her throat which brought the near swooning nurse back to the task at hand.

"Oh yes, Mr. Tyler needs his rest, but I'll escort you upstairs." She walked back down the hallway to the elevator. Momma and I followed. I wondered how or if Twitch would entertain Marin, Charity, and Frankie and whether he had on occasion entertained the nurse we followed. I couldn't worry about any of that right then.

Chapter Five

Momma Was Not in Charge

Momma and I disembarked with the nurse on the second floor. The scent of disinfectant and sickness was stronger there, but Momma didn't say anything. I made a point not to mention it. Hey, I was a vet, my patients smelled worse than this when they were healthy.

We were barely off the elevator when the charge nurse closed in on Momma. The nurse had a slight build but when she spoke her authority cast a big shadow. I knew Momma could probably take her in a wrestling match, but the nurse was certainly quicker and would leave scars.

"Hello, Mrs. Tyler, good to meet you. I'm Nurse Faison. This is my unit. I promise to use the best practices and standard of care nursing for Joseph. I know you're a nurse, too, and I heard you run a tight, efficient clinic in Bend. Here, I'm in charge."

"Momma is going to break her like a stick," Becky said.

Nurse Faison continued, "You're welcome to visit your husband now and I've arranged for a recliner to be placed in his room so that you can stay overnight if you wish. I just need your assurance you will not interfere with his care as ordered by Dr. Jonas. Do you understand, Peggy?"

Momma glared at the nurse. "Nice scrubs, little rabbits, didn't they have any with wolverines?" Momma might understand but she didn't have to like it.

Nurse Faison turned away from us and pointed to the room where we could find Dad.

Becky gasped, but didn't comment on his looks immediately.

He looked so small in his hospital bed. I wondered if even Momma would look small in a hospital bed. Then again maybe the white sheets, tubes, and machines dwarfed his existence. He breathed on his own, but a bank of monitors measured him inside. Different colored numbers flashed. His pulse, respiration, blood pressure, blood oxygen level, and possibly the S&P 500 index were recorded on the monitors by his bed. An infusion pump fed his veins and a catheter drained his bladder. Checks and balances. His skin looked pale against his baby-blue hospital gown.

After staring a while, I finally figured out why he looked so strange beyond the medical attempts to monitor and mend him. He wasn't wearing his hat. He always wore a hat, usually a freebie from the gas station or feed store. He couldn't care less about sports teams except on occasion when he allowed himself to believe in the Minnesota Twins. He had no time for the Vikings, and the Timberwolves disgusted him so much that he suggested they have an outdoor stadium. He didn't believe me when I told him Minnesota had a good women's professional basketball team. Anyway, without a hat he looked small, naked, and vulnerable.

Momma pulled a chair up close to the bed on Dad's left side. She took his hand. Maybe it was the hospital ambience or maybe the risk of losing him, but I looked at him, them both, more closely. The veins on his hand were raised and turquoise. Momma's hands were fleshier, and her veins were barely visible below the surface of her big hands. Dad had a split nail on one finger where he'd mashed it trying to build his own hydraulic wood splitter. His hands were stained and scarred from the recklessness and danger of his labors. Momma's hands were clean and pink from the precautions of her profession.

Momma was gentle and deliberate as she handled his callused paw; she didn't disturb the flow of intravenous fluids, medicine, or nutrients. For a moment I tried to imagine them in early courtship holding hands for the first time. This revelry was brief because Momma talked again.

"I could just kill you for scaring me like this. Don't you dare leave me." She kissed his hand and then pressed it against her cheek.

Leave it to Momma to threaten a stroke victim with murder for their thoughtlessness. Still, my eyes teared up as I watched her keep hold of his hand and massage it with her spoon-shaped short thumbs. She touched his hair. "Your hair is getting shaggy. How'd I let that happen? You look like a hippy."

Dad didn't open his eyes. Self-preservation. I wondered if he could hear her but chose to let her continue without an argument. It wasn't like he fought her much anyway. I wanted him to wake up and tell me an animal story about a big bear or a fox who got unexpectedly sick but it only made them stronger so that they lived a hundred years longer than all the other beasts.

I scraped another chair across the floor and sat beside him on his right-hand side. "Dad?"

He opened his eyes briefly like his lids were too heavy to keep open. I pretended they weren't leaden from drugs but were protecting him from the potential radiation in the room. I glanced over at Momma. She was crying, bawling like a baby. We sat there together avoiding eye contact with one another but staring at him.

"This is boring," Becky whispered. Leave it to Becky to expect to be entertained. "What do you think is going to happen, Lorraine?" Just when I was feeling some tenderness toward Becky, she wrecked it all and said, "You better take care of him. Don't let him down like you did me."

Neither our staring nor Momma's voice and hand massage roused him. Dad didn't awaken before a nurse asked us to leave. They needed to change his catheter and IV bags. Only one of us could stay for the rest of the morning. Of course, that part of the production fell to Momma, his leading lady.

Chapter Six

Extras in the Green Room

I hoped either Marin or Charity would have left the hospital. That was new. I'd never wished either one of them away in my life. They were both waiting for me in the lobby talking with Frankie. *Oh God, what's Frankie telling them?* Twitch was gone. Damn, I'd wanted to tell him what Warren McGerber had said to me.

Both Marin and Charity stood up when I entered the lobby. *Great.* I wanted to run. Then again, I wanted to kiss both of them. Frankie was polishing her nails. Thank heavens I had a topic. "Well, Dad is resting. He's hooked up to a half dozen monitors but he's breathing on his own. So far, Momma hasn't been kicked off the floor again, but there is a nurse who will chew Momma's ass if she tries to take over."

Marin took my hand. Again, it seemed like Charity stared wide-eyed at the gesture. I didn't know how to identify my feelings. Was I embarrassed? Scared? And why would I be either of those two things? Charity and I were done, kaput, a thing of the ancient past. I had no reason to feel any guilt or embarrassment about holding Marin's hand right then, dating Marin, and even all the lovemaking I'd done with Marin. I was allowed. I wasn't married. I was a free agent. I felt sick.

I wished they'd had follow-up questions, but they just stared at me.

Becky giggled.

"Who's up for cafeteria food?" I sounded lame.

Frankie raised her hand immediately even though she'd just binged on gas station fare.

"I'm going to talk with your momma about these insurance forms," Marin said waving that folder again.

"You know, I think Momma has family insurance through her job at the clinic. I'm under her plan until I'm twenty-six. I'm sorry I forgot."

"Oh."

"That was a dumb, insensitive thing to say, Lorraine. She looks like she's ready to serve you up a big old bowl of whip-ass!" Becky was enjoying herself at my expense.

I suppose I had just robbed Marin of the one thing she felt like she could do for our family at present.

Marin dropped my hand and glanced at her watch. "I've already had breakfast and it's too early for lunch for me. I must get back to work. I have more clients to see. Oh, before I forget, Addie sent a note for you."

I stared at Marin's face trying to assess the damage I'd done. I took the crumpled paper without reading it and stuffed it in my pocket for later. It felt like there was something I was supposed to know enough to say, but I forgot my lines or never knew them in the first place. Becky was no help. Should I have asked Marin to stay longer? I had never been in this situation before. Add to that I was worried sick about Dad. Him dying had never been real to me before.

"Catch-up later?" I asked Marin.

She flashed a look at Charity and then me. "Yeah, later." She hugged Frankie again, turned, and left.

"Where does that moment fall on the meter for awkwardness?" Charity pushed my shoulder before she took me in her arms. She took in a deep breath and let it out slowly as she held me.

"It ranks right up there with Momma seeing this woman again." I pointed to Frankie. "When Momma met Frankie the first time, she kept staring at Frankie's crotch like it was a jack-in-the-box. The 'Pop Goes the Weasel' music ran through my head." Charity laughed and pulled me tighter.

"Ha, ha, ha. Very funny, Lorraine. Your momma is just struck by my beauty," Frankie said. "Where's the cafeteria?"

"Believe me, knowing my momma if any striking was happening, she'd be doing it." I said this over Charity's shoulder with Charity still in my arms. I felt like I could have stayed in that position for the rest of my life. It was both familiar and exciting all over again.

"I think I'm going to be sick," Becky said.

"I think I'm going to find the cafeteria," Frankie said staring at Charity's and my embrace. I wondered if she would tell Marin I hugged Charity an inordinate amount of time. She walked away glancing over her shoulder as she rounded the corner into the hallway.

"Do you really want cafeteria food?" Charity said into my neck.

She smelled like strawberries, the big, fleshy ones in expensive strawberry ice cream. I can see their little seeds and imagine them having given up their lives to be in that creamy concoction, a sort of wacky fruit cryogenics, but they would never be re-animated because I planned to eat every one I could get to my mouth.

"I'm more tired than hungry to be honest." I released her and looked into her hound-dog-brown eyes.

Charity smiled and grabbed my arm. "Come with me. Do you have your cell if your momma needs to reach you or advise you or complain generally?"

"Yep."

She took my hand and led me to her truck in the parking lot. Marin's vehicle was gone; at least I didn't see it anywhere.

"Leave yours here. I'll take you back to Bend for a while. The new highway has cut the travel time in half because you can drive a modern speed. We can talk in my old studio above the garage."

"What about Frankie?" I asked. "What about your parents?"

"Somehow, I think Frankie can manage about any situation including you being gone for a while. As for my parents, they won't think anything of my truck in the yard and being back since they called me to come home. Besides, I thought you and my dad had reached some new understanding back when he made the church sanctuary for Ricky last year."

"I think we did."

"That story shocked me. Dad didn't tell me the whole thing of course," Charity said. "Mom told me it had been Dad's idea to offer the church as sanctuary to Ricky once Dad understood there were people set on killing Ricky for being queer." She hesitated and then added, "Like us."

"I still don't suppose he wants me together with you, romantically."

"We're two friends talking," she said.

I watched her walk to her truck and wondered if that was all we were. Could we ever be just that? *Where does she buy her jeans?*

I left a note for Frankie under the windshield wiper. She'd find it after foraging in the hospital cafeteria. I imagined she'd get in the truck again and sleep until I was back. Maybe a better friend would have waited for her or ran inside to ask her to join me.

I got into Charity's truck with her. I had these feelings I'd been aware of since I first saw Charity again. I was trying to name them.

"God, you're dumb, Lorraine," Becky said. "Do you need the poster of bald-headed circle people with names of feelings below their weak chins: sad, mad, glad, hornier than hell?"

I didn't like that chart. If they were children, they were all disappointed like they were cast offs from an audition for *South Park*. I couldn't ever easily find what I felt in those faces. Scared, proud—no, excited, that might be it. I ignored the feeling a while. The drive from the hospital back to Bend felt longer than it was before the new highway.

"I'm sorry about what happened on your trip to Europe." She probably knew I meant what Kelly did and she probably knew it was hard for me to say that name. I always felt like I should spit afterward—like the very utterance left poison on my tongue. "I hope there were parts of the trip too beautiful to be spoiled by anything. Did you do some painting or drawing?"

"Both." Her face broke into a radiant smile.

God, she was beautiful. I remembered the first time I had seen her at the Bend library. I was seventeen, a senior in high school. She was nineteen, finishing some college courses by correspondence. Her parents and younger sister were already living in Bend. I could easily remember Charity's auburn hair and creamy-pink skin against the backdrop of shelves of books and framed pictures of dead presidents. Her hound-dog-brown eyes looking up at me from the sketch she was making. God, she was beautiful.

"I can't wait to show you my new work. Not now of course while you're worried about your dad, but maybe some time." Charity spoke with energy and excitement. "The churches and other architecture were stunning. I saw centuries of great art. It was amazing to be somewhere where it had been a priority to commission beautiful paintings, statues, and music for whole cities. I realize much of it was made for the rich and ruling classes specifically, but what a blessing so much history and original art has been preserved for everybody to see and visit."

I think maybe right there she wanted to say we should see it sometime together, but she didn't. Maybe I just wanted her to say it. She probably remembered when she'd told me about the trip and how I had assumed I was invited until I heard she was making the trip with Kelly. My heart ached thinking about the conversation, but as she talked about specific cathedrals and museums, I smiled to hear her enthusiasm and joy. I didn't resent her for going.

"What are you so smiley about?" she asked me.

"I don't know. It's cool that we are both doing things we love. It's weird to compare the two, but maybe you feel about the same seeing great art and sketching like I feel about delivering calves or figuring out what's ailing a prize horse or bull and spaying and neutering stray cats and dogs. We're each studying and practicing what we love. That's something to be grateful for."

The gratitude I felt in my body slowly evaporated and my stomach clenched as I saw more and more

McGerber campaign signs. They were so plentiful, as if they'd reproduced from spores like fungus. I pointed to one of the signs. "Could that monster actually get elected?"

She looked at me like I should know better than to ask such a question. We lived in a state where we had elected a professional wrestler as governor; and we lived in a nation that had elected plenty of oafs as presidents. "Dad is really upset."

"I would have thought he would support McGerber on most things."

"Have you heard what he's been saying?" She glanced at me but kept her eyes on the road.

"I heard a hell of a story from him just today," I said under my breath.

"He's pledged to introduce a bill to close the Minnesota border to immigrants. He wants to put a bounty on people who don't have citizenship and jail them in work camps unless they pay to return to their home country. The man is maniacal. That's why..."

"What?"

She hesitated and said, "It feels selfish saying this to you while your dad is in the hospital."

"What? Say it."

"I'm worried about my dad."

"Is he getting dizzy on his moral high ground?" As soon as I'd said it, I regretted the words. I had gotten used to expecting the worst when it came to Grind.

"Something like that. Never mind."

"Charity, I'm sorry. That was a stupid, petty thing to say. I know your dad is trying. He provided sanctuary for Ricky when Ricky was in danger. I'll never forget that. Tell me, what's worrying you about your dad?"

"He's so conflicted. He's thinking about leaving the church."

"He can't do that!" Becky was back.

"Leaving the church? That's crazy." I was becoming a bit of an expert on crazy in my own mind.

"Mom called me to come back home even before Dad did. Mom's worried about how upset Dad is about the things McGerber is saying. McGerber makes it sound like he's got the church behind him. I've never seen Dad like this. He keeps asking Mom if he sounds like McGerber. He's embarrassed by what McGerber is saying. Well, I've seen him like this but never so focused on a man who says he's following the word of God."

"McGerber is peddling hate and fear not the word of God. Your dad sees that."

"That's just it. Dad does see it and he wants to step in but that would mean..."

"Killing McGerber?"

"No, not killing McGerber but running against him. Dad would have to give up his church."

"Crap."

"Crap," Becky said.

"I know. He loves having a congregation. He likes being there for everyone's weddings, funerals, baptisms, Christmas, and Easter. Pastors play an important role in the lives of a community. They are safety nets of sorts, every bit as much as social workers. They witness and put words to all these personal events and hopefully bring comfort to people."

"No, I mean it's crap that he should have to run. Why do men think the answer to stopping out of control men is to become one of them? It's like the Democratic Party. Why can't they put egos aside and form a coalition behind a candidate instead of tearing each other down to be the one and only?" Sometimes I wished there was somebody to mute me when I got on a tangent. Luckily, Becky was in my head.

"Sure, make this about your hatred for men," Becky said.

"I think we are a little off topic, Lorraine. Mom called me and said Dad has been fasting and praying trying to make a decision. She said he is thinking of running himself."

"I thought filing dates for fall elections ended in May."

"There was a computer glitch. He has until the end of June. That's why my dad agreed with your dad about getting an additional town hall meeting on the schedule in Bend. It would give him the perfect place to announce his candidacy. He's still deciding. He wouldn't be giving himself much time to mount a campaign. That's another reason he called me. He wants me to come home and run his campaign if he decides to run."

Well, knock me over with a feather. Charity's dad Pastor Grind was thinking of running against the hating man, McGerber. Not only that, Grind wanted his gay daughter to run the campaign. I knew Grind had been changed when he saw how festering hate and fear had pushed ordinarily kind people to wish harm against Ricky. He made the church a sanctuary for Ricky until Ricky was safe. I hadn't imagined Grind ever accepting queers altogether. Maybe I was wrong. I hoped I was wrong. *What would it mean for Charity and me if Grind accepted queers?*

"I can't picture your dad anywhere but in the pulpit."

"Me neither. He seems to think he has to be a candidate to stop McGerber."

Dumb.

We rode for a while in silence. It wasn't uncomfortable. It felt familiar and nice to be together. Those feelings came again. I was tingly.

Charity turned off the highway when we got closer to Bend. She took the curves, dips, and dives of our country roads slowly and practiced.

"I think I told you, but my dad says the guy who made our roads was either drunk or dodging gunfire. My money is on both."

Charity smiled. "It's all these lakes."

"Yeah. It's like God tossed them about like playing cards, a new one every two miles."

We were quiet a moment. "You know, there's another way to stop McGerber," I said.

"How?"

"Knock him out of the race by finding Lewis or Petey to testify to what really happened when Ricky was beat."

"I doubt Lewis or Petey will show their faces in Bend ever again. Have you heard from them?"

"No, when we last spoke, I had Dad's shotgun pointed at Lewis and Petey was scuttling across the floor like a roach trying to get out of our farmhouse. I doubt they'd contact me unless..."

"What?"

"It's probably nothing, but I have been getting some hang-up calls over the last few days. The number is blocked, and nobody says anything when I answer. I get the feeling there is someone on the other end of the line thinking about talking to me." I glanced at her and continued. "For a brief time, I thought it was you, but then I've been getting the same hang-up calls on my phone today."

"Why would either of them call you?"

"I don't know. It's probably my imagination; probably a butt dial or a telemarketer. I do think they liked it here." I sat with that thought for a moment. What was it like for Lewis and Petey? I would hate it if there were places I couldn't go for fear of being arrested. Granted there were places a person could be beaten, arrested, or outright killed for being queer. Lewis and Petey weren't queer, but they were wanted men.

"You know, I just thought of another way to stop McGerber," I said.

"Are you back to the idea of killing him?"

"No, I'm not for killing anybody. It wouldn't hurt my feelings if he died, however. I was thinking it makes more sense for your dad to throw in with the candidate who is running against McGerber than to enter the race himself, especially this late."

Charity looked at me like I'd offered her a bowl of snot soup and intestines. "Think about it, Lorraine. Then tell me you can picture my dad throwing in with this other candidate."

I did what she told me to do. I thought about Allison Jackson, the other candidate for senate in our district. I'd read some interviews—okay, Frankie read an interview with Ms. Jackson from the newspaper to me from the bathtub. Ms. Jackson sounded smart, experienced, and funny. I'd seen her picture. She was African American.

We'd reached her parents' place. I ducked under the dashboard while Charity pulled her truck into Grind's yard. I knew the drill. She would park her truck in a part of the yard out of direct view of her parents' house. I would hustle up the outside stairs to the studio apartment Charity had above her parents' garage. We had made this maneuver many times in order to have time together without Charity's dad catching us.

"I'm going over to the house. I want to see if Mom and Dad are home, give them an update on your dad, and hopefully short-circuit any spontaneous visits to the studio from them. Make yourself comfy. I'll bring back a sandwich and chips. The food may not be any better than hospital cafeteria food, but I guarantee better company."

Charity's studio apartment had always been a comfy and incredibly exciting place for me. Well, except for the time I'd hid under her bed naked and she came home with her ex-girlfriend, Kelly. Surprise.

While Charity checked in with her parents, I remained clothed. The apartment was just as I remembered it: cluttered with finished paintings, drawings, and other paintings and sketches in progress, busts and statues, bowls and vases made on the potter's wheel my dad had rigged up for Charity and likely fired in the kiln Dad had built with her. Her duffel bag was on the floor like she had dropped it off and left again.

"Lorraine Tyler, I cannot believe you are horsing around with your girlfriend when our father is incapacitated in the hospital," Becky said. "For shame."

I ignored Becky because I didn't want Charity to find me talking to myself and partly because I knew Becky was right. I continued investigating Charity's apartment.

A thin layer of dust covered everything although I suspected that Mrs. Grind had tidied the place several times over the past year. It helped me to block out Becky's nattering by imagining Mrs. Grind sitting in the apartment remembering her daughters from before they were old enough to go off to college or Europe, fall in love and have their hearts broken. Charity's younger sister Jolene had graduated with me and was now in college and engaged to be married.

I scanned the room: a galley kitchen, living room, three-quarters bathroom, an apartment sized washer and dryer stacked against one wall, and a small bedroom with a queen-sized bed. I shivered. I'd been in that bed. I wouldn't go near it today. I gravitated to the cozy couch that probably had an imprint of my butt stamped into the leather from the many times I sat there with Charity. The tingly feelings increased.

Crap, I know what this is.

"It's about time, idiot," Becky chided me.

It was only after I sat down, and Charity returned with a ham and cheese on croissants—Momma never made or bought croissants—and a can of pop, that Becky stopped talking. I listened and let my eyes examine the ceiling and corners of the room like I might see Becky aloft there. "I wonder where she went?"

"Where who went?" Charity slipped her shoes off. She wore socks she'd painted. I saw the words *trust, forever*, and *heart* before she folded her legs and feet under her and sat next to me on the couch.

"I'm going to sound looney." I inhaled my sandwich and swilled back the pop like I hadn't eaten in a long time. I hadn't.

"When has worry about sounding sane ever kept us from talking?"

Charity straightened her legs out, scooched closer to me, and put her arm around me so that my head rested against the inside of her shoulder and rise of her breast. There was probably an imprint of me there, too, from all the times I nuzzled in her arms.

"Before I tell you my newest embarrassment..."

She cut me off. "You mean that you're dating a social worker? Duh! It was obvious at the hospital. Lorraine, I'm telling you, that woman wants to own you."

"No, that isn't it. Own me?" I wondered if I had made a mistake going home with Charity. I sat up and disentangled from her arms.

"Sorry, what were you going to say?" Charity said.

Her statement irked me. At the same time, I wanted to straddle her where she sat and kiss her. I wanted to be inside her and crawl around on top of her until I'd kissed every naked inch of her, and I wanted a reciprocity agreement. I kept my bearings and remembered the social worker slam.

I had no reason to be embarrassed about Marin. I didn't need to justify myself to Charity. Hadn't she as much as owned me for those years? And hadn't Kelly owned Charity? They'd just taken a trip to Europe for heaven's sake. "Maybe, I shouldn't tell you." I crossed my arms.

"I shouldn't have made the crack about Marin. I'm sorry. I'm not used to being jealous." She put her hand on my forearm. "Please talk to me."

Charity admitted she was jealous of someone else loving me. That's new.

"I'm having this weird thing happen. I hear Becky's voice in my head like she is telling me stuff—mostly what I've done wrong or failed to do. I'm worried I might be..."

"Be what?"

"Like Becky. Maybe I'm getting sick." Vomit rose in my throat. Tears streamed down my face. It was the first time I had cried about hearing Becky's voice.

She took me in her arms again. She cuddled me into her body and pulled a Minnesota Twins throw over me. "Shhh, it will be okay. For now, just rest. Just sleep. You are safe and sound."

I hoped she was right.

Chapter Seven

Words and Nerves

When I awakened, warm, viscous drool ran down my cheek onto Charity's lap. For a moment I wasn't sure where I was. I felt someone's hands working through my jumbled curls. For a moment I thought it could be Becky detangling my hair. The sweetest least conflictual times we'd had together as sisters were when we played "beauty school dropout" and Becky tried to make my unruly hair look like a style from one of her women's magazines.

Charity touched my cheek. "You were one tired cowgirl."

I remembered where I was. The word cowgirl made me think of Marin. I sat up straight. I remembered Becky was dead. I slumped back against the couch and tried to make my voice unaffected. "Yes, Missy, I believe I was. I was also a prodigious drooler. I seem to have gotten your jeans wet."

She smiled. "That's not new."

My face reddened.

"Lighten up, Raine. I'll dry."

I sat up. My relaxed state was temporary. "What time is it? Did I miss visiting hours?" I jerked to my feet and looked out of the window to see what I could tell from the summer sky.

"Lorraine, it's okay. You only slept an hour. It's not even noon. You've still got time to visit your dad. I can drive you back to the hospital as soon as my legs wake up." She stood and stretched. I admired her jeans again.

I stood up and moved closer to the door. Was she going to say anything about the thing I told her? Maybe she was trying to get the lunatic out of the house and away from sharp objects. Crap. My mind was spinning.

"You know, Lorraine, I'm no expert about psychology," Charity began.

"I'd say she's crazier than I was. That fool is in love with you, Lorraine." Becky was back.

"Maybe Marin knows a lot more than I do and she'll tell you what she thinks when you talk with her, but I wouldn't jump to the I'm crazy card just yet. You've been through a lot." She grabbed her truck keys. "I'm surprised it isn't your momma and your sister giving you an earful about your life. For that matter, I wouldn't have been surprised if my dad had made a cameo appearance on that dramedy. Be gentle with yourself. I think you're going to be fine and Becky will quit yapping in your head eventually. You're probably still working things out."

*

I scampered out of the studio apartment and got into Charity's truck being mindful to keep my head below the front window until we were out on the road. From the floor of her truck I let my eyes follow the line of her body, feet to hair.

"As long as I'm telling you my deep dark secrets maybe I should admit I'm not certain how to be with you without being your girlfriend. I just keep thinking of kissing you, touching you."

"It's a big change for us." Charity backed out of the yard and onto the blacktop.

"So, you know what I mean?"

She accelerated away from her parents' house but pulled over onto the shoulder of the road fairly quickly. "I don't know, Lorraine. Do you mean it's like the feeling I get when I look at your lips and want to taste them and linger on them for a while?"

Christ this isn't helping, but I like it.

Becky said, "La, la, la..." I imagined her covering her ears.

"Or maybe, more accurately it is this buzzing down my legs and my palms because I'm not wrapped around you or at least touching your wild hair?"

"Yeah, that's it." My mouth was dry, and my jaw drooped. I crawled off the floor and took my seat, buckling my seatbelt quickly.

"Yeah, Lorraine. I know what you mean. I have those feelings too." She signaled and pulled her truck back on the road.

"How do people manage this?"

"Let's see, what do other people do? I bet some just give in to the feelings and have a really exciting time." She smiled and raised her eyebrows at me.

I cracked the window open for air.

"I suppose some people stay away from each other and judge themselves as having terrible, sinful thoughts." She kept her eyes on the road.

I closed the window. It had gotten chilly.

"Look, Lorraine, we love each other. We have been lovers. It's not likely that our feelings for each other just end and our bodies don't respond to each other. Our nerves haven't been cut. We haven't had any practice being together without being lovers."

"Is that how it is with Kelly? Do the boundaries seem blurry and your body reacts to what's familiar?"

"I suppose. There's a way we got used to being with each other." Charity adjusted her side mirror. "Unfortunately, with Kelly that pattern also always included one of us wandering off after some shiny thing."

I wondered if I had been Charity's shiny thing, but I didn't ask. I thought briefly of Momma and Twitch having been together briefly so long ago. Had Twitch been the shiny thing or Dad?

I hazarded a theory. "Maybe, our bodies and feelings take longer to find the edges than our language. I mean we can say we aren't together. I could say I am with Marin and my body and heart hasn't caught up to my words."

"Sounds very possible, so let's not do anything drastic like swearing off each other," Charity said.

"Okay." I noticed she hadn't eliminated giving in to the idea and having an exciting time.

"For shame, for shame." Becky was listening again.

Charity left the back roads and got on the highway that would take us back to Langston.

"You know, I had a little time to think about what you said about your dad being unlikely to throw in with that other candidate. Is it because she's a she? Or is it because she's Black?"

"Both and more, probably. Lorraine, I heard that she's Somali and probably Muslim."

"Oh." I wondered if it was true or some rumor Warren McGerber had started. Either way I didn't totally get it. To me, one religion claiming to be better than another was like warring trailer parks. What was the point? Didn't they each have enough in common to play together and take on the real evil of this world which to me seemed to be hate and indifference to suffering.

"You know she was born here, educated at the U of M. She's awfully smart and I've heard an interview. She can command a crowd. She taught in the public schools before she turned to politics."

"I agree with you. I'd vote for her, but I don't know that my dad would or could."

"I haven't heard that she's brought religion into it."

"Someone will, Lorraine. Reproductive rights will come up, abortion, gay rights, immigration, health care, welfare reform—all the hot topics that divide people instead of the parts of all those things most people could agree on."

Charity and I jawed on these political topics which squelched any tingly feelings I had, but certainly made me think of becoming a drunkard from the hopelessness. The drive to Langston went quickly. Charity dropped me back in the hospital parking lot where I'd left my truck. I spied Marin's truck parked adjacent to where Momma had parked the station wagon on part of the sidewalk and grass. That reminded me I hadn't read the note Marin gave me from Addie.

Before I could fish the paper out of my pocket, Charity hugged me and kissed me quick on the lips. She held her forehead against mine and said, "Some things are just between you and me and don't involve anyone else."

I rubbed my lips together like I was holding that kiss tightly. I hoped she was right.

She offered to come with me to see Dad, but I told her they probably wouldn't let anyone in his room except me and Momma. I got out of Charity's truck and talked with her through the open window.

"Pull up by my truck and honk your horn. Frankie is probably asleep again in there."

I slapped my hand against the door of her truck like I was shooing away a horse. If she noticed Marin's truck, she didn't let on. She waved goodbye to me as I passed from the summer air that was slightly tinged with the smell of sunbaked manure on fields through the pneumatic doors into the disinfected and overly air-conditioned air of the hospital lobby.

Marin sat in the waiting area. She had her leather boots off. She massaged one foot as she made notes in a calendar. I'd massaged those feet before myself. It made me think of Frankie. Marin's feet were about half Frankie's size. I didn't know if it would matter to me if they were bigger. I hoped not. Marin looked up like she had a detection system dialed to my frequency. She smiled and stood up.

I smiled back and walked closer to her, curious about what I'd say next.

"There you are. I've been wondering when you would show up. I called your cell."

She kissed me but not squarely on the lips because I had looked down. I fished my cell out of my pocket. Eight missed calls, only one from Marin. The rest were from a blocked number. I thought for a moment of Lewis and Petey. I didn't remember turning off my phone but supposed I had when I went up to Dad's room. Hospitals are fussy about cell phones interfering with their own electronic equipment and monitors.

"I'm sorry. I turned my phone off when I was up on Dad's floor."

Marin hugged me and kissed my cheek. "Did you sleep outside on the ground? You look awful."

No, I slept in Charity's glorious lap.

"I probably look a sight. I, uh, I..."

"Frankie told me you left the hospital without saying where you were going or when you'd be back." Marin stared at me.

I must have looked like I'd had a stroke myself. I couldn't get my words out.

"What's wrong?"

Becky was amused. "This would be funny if it weren't so depraved."

"Frankie's asleep in the truck, although she might be awake again now." Marin continued staring at me.

I figured she got that stare from doing her social work with victims and perpetrators. I might as well come clean. I didn't know if I was either one. "Nothing is wrong, really. I'm stammering because I went home with Charity and fell asleep on her couch."

"Oh, I see." Her expression froze and I couldn't read it or place it on the circle headed chart.

I swallowed hard. I wondered if Frankie had told Marin about my long embrace with Charity. I wondered if Frankie had speculated that I had disappeared with Charity. "I'm embarrassed to tell you but not because Charity and I were together or anything." *Some things are just between you and me and don't involve anyone else.* "We talked about her trip to Europe, her dad maybe opposing McGerber for our district's open senate seat, and I fell asleep. I haven't been sleeping well for at least a month. This intense summer course and finals, I suppose."

I didn't suppose June term or finals. I knew my lack of sleep was because of Becky's bellyaching in my head.

"What do you need from me, Lorraine?" She tilted her head, solicitous, but she looked forty percent sad and sixty percent mad. I'd interviewed my share of suspects as well and had some facility at reading nonverbal cues. Frankie called them "non-gerbil cues."

"Would you go with me to the cafeteria? I had a sandwich at Charity's apartment. It made me remember how hungry I am. I want to eat some protein and then go see Dad."

"You sure know how to romance a woman." She looked at her watch. "Brunch or lunch at the hospital cafeteria. Wow, I wonder what their wine selection is like."

I laughed at that. "Well, neither of us are wine drinkers so I guess we'll be okay. I doubt the hospital allows wine or beer. There's probably a fair number of people from Bend who lament that rigid policy and I dare say there have been plenty of transgressors bringing the devil's tonic into these hallowed medical halls. Dad may have a six-pack of Grain Belt cooling in his bathroom toilet tank as we speak." I took Marin's hand and kissed it. "You smell nice. I need to shower and brush my teeth. I feel like someone walked through my mouth with muddy boots."

Chapter Eight

Cafeteria Food

Langston hospital is the biggest hospital in the area, but it's small. The cafeteria wasn't very busy. I noticed a few hospital staff, dressed in pastel colors or stark white uniforms, grabbing a quick lunch. An older couple—visitors, I assumed—sat by the windows slowly eating something beige from cereal bowls and looking out into the courtyard. Becky and I'd been born in this hospital—not that I remembered. Becky had birthed Allan in the trailer home she shared with Kenny, but she'd been here at Langston Hospital for a brief time when she got sick before she was transferred to a psychiatric unit in a St. Paul hospital.

Ricky had been patched and further stabilized here at Langston Hospital after Momma and Dad had triaged and treated his most acute wounds in our living room. I can't say I had any particular warm feelings for the place in general and the cafeteria was so nondescript I doubted I'd remember the place five minutes after leaving.

I carried a plastic tray for the both of us as Marin pointed at items in the heated pans below the sneeze guard: fried potatoes, bacon, sausage, scrambled eggs, French toast, and hot oatmeal. Wow, we'd caught the tail end of breakfast. Obviously, the cook hadn't consulted the dietician or cardiac unit. Maybe the fried food was a business strategy like the dentist who gave me a coupon for an ice cream cone or small Coke at the corner drugstore after my annual check-up.

The cold pan storage counter had yogurt, dried cereal, cottage cheese, hard-boiled eggs, and anemic looking fruit salad. Another counter sported a toaster, white and wheat bread, bagels, and English muffins. Marin grabbed a bagel. I stayed with the heart attack buffet.

I joined Marin at a table away from the other diners. For a few moments I was consumed by eating. Everything tasted so good. I nearly picked up a fork in each hand but calmed myself, remembering there wasn't anybody who was going to steal my food or remove my plate before I'd finished.

"What has been happening with you, Lorraine? You look exhausted." She pointed her butter knife at my plate. "You're eating like you've been deprived of food for weeks. Haven't you been taking care of yourself at school? So help me, we may have to get a place together halfway in between so that I can take care of you properly. What's wrong?"

What's wrong? Good question. That woman wants to own you. Is this the moment to tell her about my tingly feelings with Charity and that we've had no practice not being lovers? Should I tell her about what McGerber said to me at the gas station? Or should I tell her that her girlfriend was hearing the voice of her dead sister? Oh, and her girlfriend was thinking about herself in the third person.

"I haven't been sleeping worth shit and apparently, I haven't had an appetite until this morning. The last month has been just strange. I've been so worried about it I was trying to reach Momma. I couldn't get her on the phone. That's when I called Twitch and heard from him Dad had a stroke."

"You were purposely calling your momma? Your month must have been terrifically strange." Marin slathered her bagel with cream cheese.

I looked side to side and whispered, "I've been hearing voices." I surveyed the room again like I might have been overheard. Of course, no one was as interested in my drama as I was. "Well, just one voice actually."

Becky butted in, "You're going to regret telling her, Lorraine."

"What do you mean?" Marin stared at me, but she didn't choke on her bagel or move her chair farther away. She added a slice of bacon to her bagel. She was just my kind of woman—hear distressing news? Add pork.

"I mean that I have been hearing Becky's voice in my head."

"Really?" She bit into her bagel. "What does she say?"

My throat tightened. "She talks shit about all kinds of things. She says I could have saved her."

"That's mean." Marin licked cream cheese from her fingers.

"You can't call her mean. She's dead." I was surprised that Marin didn't know the rules for discussing dead family members—only large matriarchs were allowed to acknowledge the dead had been anything other than saintly.

"Plenty of people are dead who were also mean in their life. From what you've told me, your sister Becky was sometimes mean. I doubt you're actually hallucinating. More likely you're imagining what she would say if she could talk at you."

"Charity said you'd know more about this. Why would I want Becky talking to me?" I ate a whole sausage link.

"You already told Charity?" She put down the rest of her bagel and wiped her mouth on a paper napkin.

"Yeah, shouldn't I have?" *Way to go, Lorraine. You know the etiquette for talking about dead people, but you don't know shit about how to talk to your girlfriend.*

"Of course, you can tell anybody anything about your life." Marin took up her bagel again and averted her eyes from me. "I'm just surprised is all."

I was out of my depths. I'm not a strong swimmer. "I didn't know Charity was back. I was surprised to see her. I haven't seen her since we were still together." I hesitated between each sentence like I waited for her to challenge me. She didn't.

Marin closed her eyes. I doubted it was because that bagel was so exquisite. I watched her sit there breathing slowly. When she opened her eyes again, she spoke to me in the gentlest of tones, "Lorraine, I'm sorry. I'm acting like a possessive idiot. It makes sense you wanted your momma, and it makes sense you talked to your friend, Charity. You aren't obligated to tell me things first. It's not like we're married or anything." Her lower lip rose into a pout. "Tell me more about what's been happening for you. It must have been scary."

She's such a grown-up. How'd she ever fall for me?

"I want to tell you things and I planned to tell you about the voices. I was also a little bit nervous to tell you I was hearing voices." I peered into Marin's eyes. She'd never lied to me—not that I'd ever caught. Her eyes had always drunk me in like I was the only person in the room. I saw the usual kindness there. "What if I'm getting sick like Becky was? We're twins. I'm made of the same stuff. If she got schizophrenia, I could get it too."

"Twitch is your bio dad, right? Have you ever asked him if mental illness ran in his family?" she asked.

"No, but I suspected there were a few plus size straightjackets worn by Momma's side of the family if you go back far enough."

"I'm not an expert on mental health. I know a little from graduate school and my work experience, but certainly not enough to diagnose anyone." She took her cell phone from her purse and began scrolling her contacts. She looked up at me.

Man, she's beautiful even while googling.

"I'm sorry I minimized what you said. If you are really worried that you are experiencing mental illness, I can contact someone who could help. Give me your phone."

I slid my cell phone across the table.

"I'll put Nancy, or whatever she's calling herself these days, in your contacts. I'll call her first. She's retired, but still takes a few private therapy clients. She doesn't bill insurance anymore. She lives on Little Swan not far from your farm."

"I can't afford that." That statement was like a get out of anything card in our family and the beauty of it was it had nothing to do with any actual financial calculation. We said we couldn't afford anything we maybe could afford but didn't want to do or pay for. Who could possibly argue with that?

Marin.

"How can you say you can't afford it without knowing how much it will cost?" Marin slid my phone back to me. She resumed eating. Then she added, "She's got an ancient dog. Maybe she will see you in exchange for vet work." She slapped the table.

The older couple looked over at us.

I smiled and waved.

"No, you should pay her whatever she asks. If it's important you should be willing to spend some money on it." She stared at me and I didn't speak. In my experience the first person to speak in these situations loses and pays.

"Besides, didn't you just tell me you bought a new canine anatomy textbook? That can't have been cheap. You already have all of Twitch's texts."

"It's a new edition," I said like it explained everything.

"How much does the anatomy of a dog change from year to year?"

I wanted to talk about the improved illustrations, but I wasn't going to win this battle. "Fine, I'll call this Nancy."

"Fine." Marin wiped her hands like she'd had enough cafeteria food and definitely enough of me. She stood up. "I'll call her first, so she knows to expect you."

"Fine." How often is the response "fine" a lie? I wondered. I shoveled the rest of my breakfast into my mouth and resisted licking the plate. I stood up. "I'm going up to Dad's room." I swallowed. "Do you want to go too?"

"No, I'll give you your privacy. Will you call me later?"

"Yeah." I kissed her cheek and wished I'd smelled better. "If you see Frankie in the lobby or truck, tell her I will be out soon."

Chapter Nine

Our Father

Dad was awake when I returned to his room. He saw me, put his finger to his lips to quiet me like we were coconspirators, and pointed at Momma who snored and snuffled in the army green Naugahyde recliner where she slept. Her CPAP was at the farm. I made a mental note to pick it up and bring her some fresh clothes.

Dad giggled and suppressed a cough. "Reminds me of my first chainsaw. Stihl. German company but made in America."

Tears fell from my eyes at seeing him with his own eyes open, aware, and alive. He'd attended PFLAG and paid five hundred dollars for a political rally without getting any meat out of the deal.

I quietly walked to the bed and hugged his shoulders. We'd never been a physically demonstrative family. Momma was a volcano of verbal expression and occasionally her flare-ups included a swat or a slap. Hugs were rationed out for deaths and births and maybe for winning some big award. I'd probably never know for certain.

Dad's shoulders felt bony like his muscles had wasted away into the sheets and mattress of his hospital bed. I knew him to be strong in every sense of the word. Maybe I faulted him for not defying Momma more often, but he had been married to her for twenty years now. Who in their right mind wouldn't call him a strong man?

Of course, I had some questions about whether I was in my right mind, but I didn't tell Dad. I wanted to tell him. I could trust him to tell me the truth—whether I should be as worried as I felt. I wanted to tell him Warren McGerber had as much as confessed to me that he beat and sexually assaulted Ricky and he had thoughts of doing the same to other people he termed *freaks*. Freaks like me, Charity, Marin, Ricky, Russ, and Frankie.

I didn't tell him. He was in a hospital bed recovering from a stroke. It wasn't the time to burden him with my neurosis or the problems of the world. I hugged him and whispered into his neck that I loved him.

"Yah, yah." He choked and teared up. His nose ran. He loved me too. Choking up was worth three, four pages typed, single spaced, gobbeldygook, mushy stuff for us Scandinavians. We were named Tyler now, but our name had been converted on the whims of the clerks at Ellis Island. All Dad could tell me for sure was that in the homeland our name had begun with a T.

I released him to my mundane inquiry. "Did you get any sleep?"

"You know how it goes in hospitals. No true rest with the odd noises and intermittent poking and prodding. Christ, it's like they want you to run out of here. I shouldn't say that." His face reddened. "They've been awfully nice."

I knew he would have been nothing but kind to his caregivers. He probably hated to inconvenience them and would have done the work himself if he could. The intrusion and embarrassment of being catheterized alone probably put him to shame. He was a strong but private man.

Momma roused as Russ, Ricky, and Frankie came into the room. I wondered where Justin was, but I didn't ask. It shocked me that the nurses were allowing so many visitors at once. Maybe they were on break or in the lobby with Twitch.

Becky was finally bothered by something other than me. "There are too many people in his room, Lorraine. This isn't good."

"Oh, you got my message." Momma struggled out of the recliner and took Ricky into her arms. She ignored Russ and I think she hissed at Frankie. Momma had found Ricky at the junior college when she was getting her nursing degree. Ricky was there studying cosmetology. Momma brought him home to meet me and straighten out her queer daughter. Little did she know she'd doubled the queers in our house when she invited Ricky to live with us.

Momma loved Ricky. She even tolerated that Ricky lived with and loved Russ. For some reason gays were more acceptable than lesbians for Momma—maybe it was their surrender into being entertaining stereotypes sometimes.

Ricky loved Russ. Russ had been another target in Momma's effort to reprogram me by bringing home a man to properly scratch my itch. No itches were scratched, but he repaired and maintained our vehicles for free. Russ, Ricky, and I were good friends. They lived together in a huge farmhouse that Russ shared with his mom, Ruth, who has MS, Kenny, Ramona, and Allan. Between the lot of them Russ and Ramona's mom had good care in her own home and Allan had a house full of people who looked out for him.

I counted myself lucky to have added Frankie to the crew. I appreciated that I had this whole posse of people who allowed me to find my own relief for any itches I had.

"I brought my best scissors, Peggy," Ricky said and then he turned to Dad. "Peggy said I needed to cut your hair before you are mistaken for a hippy draft dodger whatever that is."

"He's never dodged a draft in his life, especially if it was Grain Belt." Twitch entered the hospital room and the party.

"It's good to see you boys." Dad smiled and waved at Ricky and Russ. He bowed his head to Frankie. "The beautiful Frankie." He turned to Twitch and stuck out his tongue. "It's even good to see your ugly mug, Twitch." Dad greeted everyone as best he could from a hospital bed with tubes and whatnot. "No need to put yourself to any trouble on my account. I don't get any better looking than this."

Dad had let Ricky mess with his hair and nails when Ricky lived at our farm. Dad loved Ricky too. It was one of the worst nights of Dad's and my life when we found Ricky tied to a fence line near our farm. He'd been beaten, bloodied, broken and near dead, and we had to face that it was possibly one of our friends or neighbors who did it. Dad and Momma had saved Ricky's life, treating him quickly and getting him to this very hospital like they did.

Ricky liked to cook and was always asking Momma to teach him things like how to make gravy. He fiddled with my hair sometimes and gave me dating advice. He'd met Marin and saw she was flirting with me before I noticed it myself. He was like a replacement sister. It seemed pretty natural to have him in the hospital room with us.

The noise of our party must have reached the nursing desk. Nurse Faison didn't know all the connections between us and if she did, she was not impressed. She about blew a gasket when she came in and found Dad's bed surrounded with visitors, Ricky cutting Dad's hair, and Momma checking in with Russ on the progression of his mom's MS. Twitch stood by Momma. Frankie was scanning Dad's chart which she had lifted from the nursing cart as the nurse addressed our riotous behavior.

Nurse Faison told us in no uncertain terms to get our sorry asses out of Dad's room. Ricky could finish the haircut, but the rest of us should go to the lobby and think about what we'd done.

Frankie's eyes narrowed and she purred to the nurse. "Ooh, I like you. You're beautiful *and* mean."

"Could be worse, she could be your dental hygienist," Momma said to Russ as she harrumphed out of the room and called the elevator to take us back to the first floor.

"Thanks for coming," I said to Russ.

"More importantly, do you have a man-god named Justin staying at your house?" Frankie took Russ's arm.

Russ eyed Momma. Momma was preoccupied with digging in her purse and yapping to Twitch about something. She was probably looking for her notebook. Momma liked to keep a registry of events meant for retribution by God or Momma herself. She made the lists in a cheap spiral bound notebook with a No. 2 pencil tied to the silver wire. Her current cache of Biblically themed writing instruments had a series of Old Testament instances when God "smote" somebody or other. Maybe she'd make a note to sew a voodoo doll of Nurse Faison. More likely she'd remembered one of my legions of failures and shortcomings and wanted to jot it down. Or maybe she'd let Becky read the list into my ear later in the day.

Russ ignored Frankie's question and whispered to me, "I'm glad I got a chance to talk to you away from Ricky."

"Why?" I asked. "Did Ricky remember anything?"

"No, not much. He keeps having a dream about a half-moon shaped tattoo. It's not that, but it's what maybe happened."

"What happened?"

"Nothing, at least I don't think anything really happened." He glanced at Momma and Twitch and then whispered to me. "He's got it in his head that Lewis Gaus is back in the area and trying to kill him. I called Justin to come over for a few days. He can help me watch Ricky."

"Justin can help you watch Ricky, and I can watch Justin. Symmetry, you got to love it," Frankie said.

"Crap. Did Ricky see Lewis?" I asked Russ.

"He says a guy in a dark-green truck tried to run him off the road and the guy looked like Lewis."

I wasn't sure what to say. I didn't want to worry Russ and Ricky unnecessarily, but I also didn't want to be foolish by minimizing the new information.

I didn't get a chance to say any more to Russ because Ricky came up behind us more quickly than I had expected. He'd taken the stairs. He had his tackle box of beauty supplies under his arm. He pinched Russ's behind and then slipped under his arm on the opposite side from Frankie. The big man cuddled Ricky like a man size lovie, which he was.

"Your dad fell asleep while I was cutting his hair. I only finished one side before that nurse kicked me out of the room and barred me from performing cosmetology in the hospital unless I call her for permission. Then, she refused to give me her number." Ricky smiled and nuzzled into Russ.

"Oh yeah? This was the third time Momma has been kicked out of Dad's room," I told them.

Twitch excused himself to get something from his truck. The rest of us went into the lobby.

*

Momma sat in a waiting room chair scribbling in her notebook. Once we were closer, she addressed us as if we were attending a meeting she had called.

"Sit. We need a plan." She licked her thumb and went back a page in her notebook. "If I heard you right Lewis and maybe that Petey are back in the country."

"Remind me again, who are Lewis and Petey?" Frankie whispered to me, but Momma heard her.

"They were McGerber's minions and tried to remove this sweet boy's wires from his jaw early," Momma said. "Try to keep up, Frankie."

Ricky gasped. He hadn't heard anyone confirm his sighting of Lewis and of course he shuddered when anyone brought up his trauma.

"Did you see him, too, Peggy?" Ricky asked Momma and then glanced at me.

"No, I wouldn't know him from Adam, but Russ told Lorraine you saw him." Momma looked from one face to another in our band of ruffians. "That's enough for me to want to have a plan."

Momma always had a plan. Sometimes, she had a plan with corresponding equipment and a matching outfit. I waited. It wasn't like she needed an invitation to boss everyone around. She just looked back and forth between us, her anxiety increasing.

"Momma, what are you suggesting?" I asked.

Nothing.

I was against the idea, but I said, "Are you going to call Sheriff Scrogrum?"

"Scrogrum?" Frankie giggled.

Momma glared at Frankie. "Screen door on a submarine. Useless. I'll probably call him so he can pick-up the pieces after the real work is done, but I don't think we can hold out for him to be effectual and helpful. Those investigators from the state crime lab are gone."

That was a shame. Someone had nicknamed them Mumble and Shuffle. They were trained investigators our County had on loan from the state crime lab for a few months. They'd helped gather evidence and tie up some of the loose ends when the hate crime was perpetrated against Ricky. No matter. They were gone. We were left with Sheriff Scrogrum.

Bend, like most small towns in Minnesota, had multiple churches and hardware stores but not enough money or crime to warrant a police force or private security company. The County rationed law enforcement out to the small towns based on need. They wouldn't see Lewis and Petey being back in town as enough of a threat to warrant any investigation or protection. Oh, how I wished we were in a Netflix drama setting and had some retired lawman from a metropolis who came to Bend to exorcise his personal demons, but also solve every local crime with speed and efficiency. No such luck. We had Sheriff Scrogrum—a second generation law officer with two years' training from a technical school.

Momma still hadn't announced her plan.

"Momma, what are you thinking of doing?" She probably wouldn't tell me but at least I could say I asked. Momma had her own way of managing problems and she didn't ask for permission or even help most of the time. That day she didn't give any orders or hustle or bustle. She just sat there looking between us.

"Momma?" *Was she having a stroke too?*

She began crying. She put her face in her hands. "I don't know. I thought I'd know by the time we were sitting here, but I don't know."

"Oh God, you broke Momma, Lorraine," Becky said.

Terrific. Now I was really scared. I had planned to ask Momma for help because I was hearing Becky's voice, Dad was sick in the hospital, and now I'd learned that Ricky and I might be in danger from Lewis, Warren McGerber acted like he could do whatever he wanted, and Momma didn't have a plan for any of it. Panic coursed through me.

Just then, Twitch came back into the lobby from his truck. He sat next to Momma. He put one hand on her back as she sobbed. I noted it was his left hand—not his dominant hand. He could still do some work if Momma were to bite off the hand at the wrist. She didn't bite or yell. She looked up at Twitch and smiled. He handed her his bandana kerchief and a sandwich wrapped in waxed paper. He'd made my momma a sandwich. Apparently, that was what he'd retrieved from his truck.

Momma wiped her nose on the kerchief and sniffed the sandwich.

"It's peanut butter and grape jelly. I realized when I got home that I don't buy many groceries. I eat at the diner most days. It was this or ketchup on crackers." Twitch smiled in a bashful way I didn't know that I'd seen before. "Ketchup on crackers seemed more of an evening entrée."

"Aw, that's so sweet." Frankie dabbed tears from her eyes.

"It's perfect." Momma wiped her face again and unwrapped the sandwich and took a bite.

Twitch had cut the sandwich diagonally.

"Now what's going on here?" Twitch looked at the rest of us. "Hi, Frankie. You're looking...sensitive."

Frankie blushed but then blew a kiss at Twitch which Twitch pretended to catch in his hand and placed his hand against his heart.

"It looks like Lewis and Petey are back in the area," I said.

Russ jumped in. "That rat bastard tried to run Ricky off the road."

"Damn it," Twitch said. He looked at Momma, but she didn't chastise him for cussing.

"Ricky, are you sure you saw Lewis?" I asked.

"Yes. He was driving a dirty, dark-green truck. I swerved to get away from him and almost ran off the road." Russ cuddled Ricky under his arm again.

"Did Lewis try to run you off the road? Or did you think you saw Lewis and get scared and almost run off the road?" I knew I was being a poop, but it seemed important to get the facts right.

Ricky looked irritated at first but took a moment to think through my question. "I saw someone who to me looked like Lewis driving a green truck. I panicked and almost drove off the road. He didn't exactly drive me off the road. Maybe he would have. Don't forget what he did to us, Lorraine." He shook his finger at me.

"I won't." I couldn't. I thought about that day every day and my startle reflex still had a hair trigger on account of it. "I watch for him, too, since it happened." I held eye contact with Ricky. We belonged to this lousy club of people who had been terrorized by Lewis and Petey under the direction of Warren McGerber. I think we both wanted to dissolve the club and never add another member.

Twitch touched my shoulder. "Has Lewis or Petey come near you?"

I shook my head. Twitch turned to Ricky. "What happened exactly, Ricky?"

"Okay, so maybe I drove into the ditch and back onto the pavement, but when I looked in my rearview mirror, he had turned his truck around and was following me. I drove home but he didn't drive into the yard."

"Don't you think that's weird?" I asked.

"I think it's diabolical," Ricky said.

I was confused. "I mean, why not follow you to your house if his plan is to hurt you? Why call me?"

Twitch took his hand away from Momma's back and stood up. "He's calling you?"

Shit, why'd I let that slip. "Twitch, I don't know for sure it's him. The idea of it being him just came to me since I've been home. I'm getting hang-up calls from a blocked number. It's not Charity."

"I don't like the sound of any of this." Twitch flashed a look at Momma and came closer to me.

I had my suspicions about Lewis ever making up for his wrongs but for some reason I said, "Maybe he wants to talk or help us get McGerber."

Russ said, "Lorraine, you're assuming Lewis is logical and organized. Maybe he's not. Maybe he's biding his time to get up the courage to strike."

I thought about McGerber's venomous words from that morning. "Maybe." I refused to repeat his words particularly within Ricky or Russ's hearing.

"I'm siding with Russ. Lewis may not be acting rational. Everybody needs to watch out for him and call the sheriff if you spot him," Twitch said. "Lorraine, Peggy, maybe you should stay with me until the sheriff catches those guys."

Weird.

Momma didn't say anything. Weirder.

In keeping with the already weird trend, I spoke up and offered sanctuary to Momma. "You can stay with Twitch or vice versa." It was strange making the suggestion. I knew I should have asserted my solemn pledge about some safety precaution I would take for myself, but I didn't know what that precaution would be.

"Momma, I don't think it falls to you to solve this or make a plan." Maybe I was getting to be a grown-up too. "Ricky and I will keep our eyes open for Lewis." I motioned toward the whole group. "Our posse will help us be safe. I'll check with Addie if she's heard from Petey." Petey had been Addie's boyfriend. "She's still at the girls' ranch. Momma, Addie is graduating this month, but she'll stay at the ranch until she has a more permanent living situation."

I remembered the note Marin had given me from Addie but couldn't bring myself to read it and possibly bring more worry to so many people who were already scared. I focused on Momma. "Momma, you be with Dad. That's the only job you should be worrying about right now. Your plate is full."

I turned to Twitch. He had sat down again next to Momma and placed his hand on her back like it was the most natural gesture in the world.

"Are you staying here a while?" I asked.

He nodded.

"Good. Thank you." I turned back to Momma again. "Are you going to be okay if I leave?"

"Are you going back to school already?" Momma asked.

"No, but I'm leaving the hospital for a while to gather some information about Lewis and Petey. I'll stay here if you need me, Momma."

"You go, Lorraine, you're not that useful anyway." She turned to Twitch and placed her hand on his knee. "Joseph must be mightily doped up. You know what he told me. He told me that if anything happens to him you promised to marry me. Crazy, isn't it?"

I looked at Twitch. He smiled but didn't answer.

Russ, Ricky, Frankie, and I left Momma and Twitch in the lobby and headed out of the hospital, I supposed, each lost in our own thoughts about what we would do next. I walked to my truck. Finally, I read the note from Addie.

Petey is back for me. I'm so excited. Can't wait to tell you about it. Lewis is around too. Come see me. Hugs, Addie.

Crap.

I got in my truck with a plan to drive to see Addie. Before I got there or had a chance to ask Frankie if she was coming with me or going with Ricky and Russ, I got a text from Marin saying the counselor, Nancy or whatever name she was using now, could see me now if I could come there right away. *Great. As if I don't have enough to do.*

The thought of blowing off therapy got bigger and heavier in my head. I was about to back out when Marin texted me back with the address and a very sexy picture of herself peeking out from under the covers of her duvet. *Crap. We're overdue for hide-and-seek.*

I texted Marin to let the therapist know I was on my way. I needed to keep my word to Marin. Frankie followed on my heels asking me why I didn't ask any questions about Justin. Could we see him at Ricky and Russ's house? Possibly another hundred questions I didn't have time, interest, or intention of answering.

"Can Frankie bunk at your place tonight?" I asked Ricky and Russ.

Frankie squealed and danced in the parking lot. She got her bags from my truck and put them in Russ's truck.

Ricky jumped at the chance to work on Frankie's hair and makeup, but maybe with less enthusiasm than he would have had if he weren't worried that Lewis and Petey hid somewhere ready to silence him. I pitied Russ. There would be no sleep in their household tonight between the worry and the slumber party.

"What about you, Lorraine?" Ricky asked.

"Yeah, where are you going? Are you staying at the hospital or your farm tonight?" Frankie asked. "Or are you staying with Marin? Or Charity?"

"No," I said. Then I wondered why I wasn't staying with one of them.

"There's room for you to stay at our house, too, Lorraine," Russ said.

"I might see you later. I'm going to see a therapist," I mumbled inaudibly.

"What?" The question may have been asked by one or all of them.

"I have an appointment to meet with a therapist. Go ahead, make your jokes." I waved my hand for them to bring it on.

"Why would we joke about that?" Ricky said.

"It's about time, Lorraine. My therapist told me weeks ago you needed to be seeing somebody," Frankie chimed in.

"I see this lesbian therapist named Nancy but sometimes she asks me to call her other names," Ricky said. "It's made a big difference in my nightmares." Russ pulled Ricky close.

"Well, thank you all for your support. Jeez." I didn't feel as offended as I made myself sound. I also didn't share that I was likely going to see the therapist Ricky had seen. I was relieved they didn't think the idea was stupid. We went our separate ways.

Chapter Ten

You Can Call Me Mickey

The retired therapist Marin recommended lived within good shoes, bug repellent, and walking distance from our farm although I'd never heard of her before. Her cabin was tucked into the northwest corner of Little Swan Lake. Her choice of home meant more to me than any degrees she might have. She must appreciate beauty to have chosen and afforded that spot. Her driveway wound through overgrown bushes and tall grasses. The lower branches scratched against my truck exterior. I laughed, thinking the scraping against my truck couldn't hurt and would possibly improve the paint job's character, like I drove encased in an abstract impressionist's creation. I would try to remember the comparison to share with Charity.

It was afternoon and the heat of the day brought humidity, the churr of cicadas, buzzing flies, and chirping birds. Summer sun and a cornflower-colored sky peeked between the swaying tree canopy. A red fox scampered across the trail. I hit my brakes hard to stop in time and parked to watch the patch of tangled foliage where he'd disappeared as if by some miracle he'd present again, walk out into the open, and introduce himself, tell a story, or ask a question. I wanted to see him more closely.

"That was something," I said to the empty truck cab.

"Leave it to you, Lorraine, to marvel at an overgrown rat." Becky was back.

"Foxes are not rodents. They are part of the same family as dogs and wolves."

"I don't like dogs any better. It was you and Dad who brought home those filthy four-legged flea and tick buses."

"You will remember, Kenny kept dogs, Becky."

"His only flaw."

"Yeah, right. More importantly, why are you talking to me?"

"Ask the shrink. I'm surprised you'd go for such balderdash."

"I'm shocked anyone still uses the word balderdash." Balderdash? Really? Becky never could swear worth shit. I always attributed that one failing to her church brainwashing and her unending trajectory toward sainthood. "If you'd shut your beak, Becky, I wouldn't have to go see this counselor."

Becky stopped talking for a moment. Instead, she hummed.

The counselor's cabin came into view, framed by the blue-green water of Little Swan Lake. I hadn't even begun being shrunk and already I felt impatient. I needed to be done with therapy, talk with Addie, get some dinner, and visit Dad again. I wondered what Charity was doing. Would Marin be expecting me at her house later in the evening?

"I blame you, Becky, for me having to do this therapy thing. I really don't have time for this."

"Is that any way to speak to your dead sister? You owe me, Lorraine. I was robbed."

"What's it going to take, Becky? How do I get free of your haunting?"

"You'll find out. Just don't let that therapist say anything bad about our family." She was quiet then. I felt no relief knowing she said I'd find out. If anything, I felt more dread.

I parked my truck alongside a green Subaru wagon. A white woman with graying hair came out of the cabin. Hands on hips she smiled broadly at me. She was older than Momma but not as tall—Momma being the measure of all authority. She was dressed in a blue, loose-fitting linen tunic, khaki capri cargo pants, and hiking boots. Marin had told me that Nancy bowled on our team—she was lesbian, and her wife was a famous interior design consultant who traveled a lot. I wondered if she was at the cabin today. A gray-black, medium-sized mutt of a dog stood beside her. She talked to the dog and the rheumy eyed mutt seemed to nod at intervals but didn't bark.

"Hello. You Lorraine?"

"Yep, I take it you're Nancy."

"Call me Mickey."

"Why would I do that if your name is Nancy?" I walked closer to her. Was this the same counselor Ricky was seeing or not?

"I've always wanted a nickname. Never had one. Besides, would you want to be called Nancy?" She held the door to the cabin open for me to enter in front of her.

She made a fair point, but it wasn't for me to confirm or deny. "My first girlfriend called me Raine. I liked being called Raine."

Mickey, the dog, and some squeaky flatulence followed me into the cabin. I assume the dog provided the gas but didn't ask.

"Raine is a fine name," Mickey said. "Sounds like something from a romance novel."

It was. I knelt by the dog, breathed through my mouth. "Who is this fine, smelly hound?"

"That's Tumor."

"Tumor? Auspicious name. Hopefully, it hasn't proven itself prophetic."

"Not yet, anyway." She moved toward a seating area.

I palpated the dog's abdomen from habit and practice. Damn. I would need to tell Mickey some things about Tumor later.

"Raine, I was an unplanned pregnancy. My mother had four other children already in school when I came into being. For better or for worse she told me she had called me a tumor with legs and four-eyes in the early days of her pregnancy. She was quick to add her attitude had changed when I was out of the womb. She no longer regretted my existence. Somehow, verse two was harder to remember than the catchy phrasing of verse one."

"Are you supposed to tell me such personal things?" *Am I supposed to challenge what my therapist can or cannot say to me?* These were uncharted waters.

"No, I'm supposed to meet with you at a beige walled clinic, check your insurance card, and see you once every two weeks reporting what you tell me to an insurance company. Your choice." She shrugged. "I only take the clients I want now, and I say what I want. I won't physically or emotionally harm you or attempt to seduce or exploit you. I will be honest, kind, and I will meet with you in the pristine beauty of this lake cabin setting if that's agreeable to you."

I reached out my hand. "Nice to meet you, Mickey."

"One other thing about Tumor. I purposely named her that just as I deliberately chose her from a litter of eight gyrating fur babies. This dog was enormously wanted." She smiled.

Mickey sat on the leather loveseat and I sat on the matching couch. I relaxed more as my body sank into the cushions and cradled me. There were cans of pop and sparkling water on a tray resting on a steamer trunk repurposed as a coffee table. Tumor did several turns on her pink chenille rug beside Mickey's seat. Finally, the dog settled down in a fog of released gases and her eventual dreams.

"Another thing, I should tell you I met your sister Becky when she was at the hospital in Langston." Mickey stared at me waiting for my response. Again, I was surprised she could tell me, but Mickey ran her own party.

"I'm telling you this because you may have some feelings about that or questions for me. I won't discuss your sister with anyone over breakfast at Will's Diner or over deep-fried cheese curds at the Lake Tavern, but I will answer your questions if I can and tell you things to help you in your current struggles. Of course, what I say is my opinion not some type of holy scripture."

This eventuality, meeting someone who had been on Becky's treatment team, had not occurred to me. Questions flooded my head, but I started simply, "I'm hearing Becky's voice in my head. The doctors said she had schizophrenia. We're twins."

"I see," she said. "There's a lot of information in those sentences. I hate to sound like a TED talk performer, but you and I will have to unpack what you said and examine each part of it and not take the whole chunk as fact."

"Fact. I'm hearing Becky's voice in my head. It started a few months ago."

"Yes, Marin told me what you described. It must feel very unsettling."

"You think? Becky was a pain in the ass talking at me when she was alive. Now, she's in my head talking shit. I hope you don't mind if I cuss." I couldn't believe how wound up I was.

"I invite it. Our body knows how to tell what it needs. Our mind is part of our body and sometimes we use words, even swear words to express the complexity and intensity of what we feel. Cuss away!"

"I didn't want to come here," I said, looking at Mickey's face for her reaction.

"You're in good company. Lots of people wouldn't go to a therapist, a stranger, and talk about private things. The whole idea sounds crazy."

I laughed to hear her say the word crazy. "I'm afraid that I'm crazy like Becky was. I'm afraid I have schizophrenia."

Mickey slowly nodded as she listened to me. "Do you think I have schizophrenia like Becky did?" There. I'd asked the question and asked it of someone who might actually know.

"Like I said, I met your sister. I'm not convinced Becky had schizophrenia so I wouldn't diagnose you as having schizophrenia either." Mickey stared at me.

My body tensed. "What do you mean you aren't convinced Becky had schizophrenia? They were treating her for schizophrenia."

"I believe you. I also believe the treatment team was doing the best they could with the information they had."

She looked at me but didn't seem ashamed of what she'd just admitted.

"They gave us a handout on schizophrenia." I felt stupid the moment the words left my mouth. Was I saying being given a handout made it fact? "Dad called schizophrenia a big wheelbarrow of a disease where doctors threw things they couldn't explain."

Mickey didn't say anything. She didn't defend the hospital staff or herself. Meanwhile, I was getting more and more heated. I couldn't believe how anger and resentment welled up inside and spread tension to my every muscle and tendon. I thought about Becky being sick and being scared she was already dead or would die and dealing with hospital people.

"God damn it, the doctors, nurses, and social workers rationed out information like it was top secret, something needed for an overseas war effort. We didn't know anything. We depended on the doctors to tell us what was happening. At first, they didn't say shit but when her time was up at the hospital...then they fell over themselves telling us what *we* needed to do."

I stood up. One of my feet was asleep from holding so much tension. The needle and pins sensation made me feel weak in the knees and I nearly toppled over. Once I had my balance and feeling in my foot, I paced. I blew air out of my mouth as I organized my racing thoughts. I'd never said any of this to anyone, but it felt true and real and I didn't care what Mickey thought or Becky said. I didn't know these thoughts were pinballing around in my head.

"The hospital staff said, 'Watch her take her meds because she won't want to.' We were conscripted to monitor her medication compliance and we were authorized to bring her back to the hospital if she got 'increasingly religiously ideated and dangerous.'" I used air quotes and my most snotty voice. "Shit, Becky was always religiously ideated. She was raised and praised to be religiously ideated."

I stopped pacing and talking for a moment, my mind like a computer pulling up and spitting out the verbiage from social workers, nurses, doctors, and Becky herself which I had heard and resented. I sat down again on the couch.

"You know what Becky told me that day, the day she died? She said she didn't like taking the meds because when she took them, she couldn't hear God's voice so clearly." I wagged my head and used the snottiest Becky imitation I could muster. I was so pissed.

"It isn't uncommon for people to be hesitant about taking psychiatric medications," Mickey said calmly. "The reluctance to take medications goes right along with the reluctance to see yourself as mentally ill. Who would want to be considered mentally ill? There's stigma and misunderstanding. The medications can have debilitating side effects."

"Becky was dull and stiff when she first came home from the hospital. She didn't seem like herself."

"Some side effects go away, some don't, some even worsen. People get damaged livers and kidneys. Some people get diabetes. For some people, the cure feels worse than the disease. Add to that there isn't a cure like we normally think of it. There's recovery, but there's no cure for some illnesses."

The two of us had dueling monologues: hers about mental health generally and mine about Becky specifically.

I pulled at my hair as I ranted. "Later, Becky was frantically cleaning and praying and up at night. Kenny eventually told us that. What was the point of keeping her in a hospital and giving her those medications she didn't want if...?"

"If she wasn't cured? If people weren't sure what she had or what to do? If she might kill herself anyway?" Mickey threw all the things I was thinking out in the open like they were clay pigeons, but she didn't shoot one of them out of the air or seem defensive.

"Yeah, all those things. What was the point given what happened?" Tears came to my eyes as I pleaded with Mickey for answers.

"I don't like you talking about this with her," Becky said more quietly than her usual patter. Surprised to hear Becky again I think I looked to the ceiling. If Mickey noticed she didn't say anything.

"Mistakes are easier to see looking back than predicting the future," Mickey said. "Of course, no one knew for certain that Becky would go off her medications and certainly no one knew she'd do what she did. Still, it must have been maddening to be kept in the dark about someone you love and at the same time be commanded to manage her care out of the hospital."

"You're damn right it was." My fists clenched and spittle flew from my mouth as I talked. "Kenny was useless, but no surprise there. Momma…"

"Tread carefully, Lorraine. She'll know what you say about her," Becky said.

"Was that Becky?" Mickey asked.

"Did you hear her too?" My face flushed with embarrassment. "No, of course you didn't. I'm sorry."

"You don't have to apologize, Lorraine. You didn't insult me suggesting I heard the voice too. I just noticed you look up quickly like you heard something and were searching for the source."

"Yeah, but the source is in my head, right?"

"It seems so to you. Let's set aside the voice for a moment. You started to say something about your momma." Mickey didn't miss much.

"I should have known to watch Becky. Becky told me as much."

"What about your mother?" Mickey said.

"Oh nothing." I glanced at Mickey to see if she'd let it pass. "Isn't it a cliché to blame the mother in therapy?" I wiggled in my seat.

"I'm not looking for someone to blame or for you to blame. I just want to hear what happened. You started to say something about your momma."

Mickey wasn't going to let it slide.

"It's just... Momma usually takes charge of everything. She would rule the world if she could get away with it. She definitely rules our family." How should I explain without sounding like a whiney, blaming jerk? "Momma made it very clear that Becky was her favorite. I just wonder why she didn't take over and run things for Becky, force-feed her those medications. If anybody could've... Of course, Momma had to work."

I remembered what Becky had said as I was getting out of the truck for this therapy session. *Don't let her say anything bad about our family.* "Just so you know, Momma had a lot on her plate. She was barely recovering from thinking Becky was buried somewhere on Kenny's pig farm."

"You were all recovering from worry I suppose?" Mickey raised her eyebrows like she dared me to contradict her. "As you said your momma was working and worrying about Becky."

I smiled picturing Momma and me traipsing through the woods spying on Kenny. "We were so certain Kenny had possibly killed Becky especially after I told Momma and Dad about the bruises Becky had on her arm and how Kenny had grabbed me rough one time. Combine that with learning Becky stayed at a shelter for battered women for a time. We all thought he killed her and buried her, but none of us would say it out loud. We just each prepared and planned like it was true."

"Yours isn't the only loving family to feel the need to take care of business no matter how unpleasant the tasks," Mickey said. "What was your theory?"

"We figured Kenny had killed Becky and buried her on the pig farm. That's why he got rid of his hunting dogs. He couldn't chance them getting her scent and digging her up in the spring. We figured he'd move her body. Momma, she can be a fabulous actor, she told him this big story that Dad was bringing the good hunting dogs over to his farm to search for Becky. Momma had bought night vision binoculars to watch Kenny. She even packed snacks." I laughed at the lunacy of it. Mickey did, too, to her credit.

"Momma and I hid in the bushes and talked on walkie talkies like...like friends."

"You and your momma? Friends."

"Yes. We were sick thinking that Becky might be dead, but we had to know. So, we watched Kenny from the edge of the woods." I shook my head still incredulous to the whole situation we endured. "Sure as hell, Kenny dug up a body. It wasn't Becky, but we didn't know that right away. Momma chased after Kenny and that body. It was in a blue-and-red tarp. It was Kenny's dad, not Becky. He'd been sickly but probably died from the poison of his own soul. Kenny had hidden the body so his ma would still get old man Hollister's social security check. Idiot. His ma was legally entitled to money from his share already."

"How did you find out it was Kenny's dad and not Becky?"

"Momma caught Kenny. She did it driving backward. Momma can't back up or back down worth shit, but she maneuvered her tank of a station wagon down the driveway and cut off Kenny's path like she was a precision driver." Tears again came to my eyes as I pictured the race.

"You're proud of your momma?"

"Huh. Yeah, I guess I am."

"You don't blame your momma for Becky's death?"

I turned my head from side to side—probably looked like a cow. "All that time we were spying on Kenny, Becky was at our other neighbor's place getting sicker by the minute. She was alive. When we found her, we got her to the hospital. The hospital folks treated her, and she came home, and she died."

"So, it's Becky's voice you hear?" Mickey shifted positions. "What does she say to you?"

"She gives a running commentary on my life, but she also zings me."

"Zings you?" Mickey sat forward like she was more interested in my story.

"Yeah, she says things like I could have saved her and it's my fault that her son Little Man—we have to call him Allan now—is growing up without his mother. She says it would be ironic if I flunked out of vet school after fighting so long and hard to get there." I flatly listed Becky's most recent predictions and accusations.

"She seems to zing you with what I'd guess are some of your biggest fears and challenges. How painful."

I didn't say anything.

Mickey said, "I remember reading how you were faced with an impossible situation the day Becky killed herself. You saved Little Man, Allan, didn't you?"

"Yes, but…"

Mickey cut in. *Rule breaker.* "Allan would have died if you hadn't acted so quickly and decisively. Isn't that right?"

Mickey knew the story. Surely, she knew I failed to save Becky. "Yes, but in the time it took me to get him to safety, Becky killed herself."

"For God's sake, did you dillydally taking him to safety or did you hurry?"

I'd have liked to brain her for the insult of such a question, but I stopped a moment to remember. "No, I ran as fast as I could. Once I got Little Man a safe distance away, I went back for Becky."

"You were on your own, Lorraine. You didn't have anyone to help you? Like you said Kenny was useless and for some unknown reason your momma hadn't taken control of running Becky's life after the hospitalization. You haven't even mentioned your dad's role in all this." Mickey lowered her head but kept her eyes locked with mine.

"I don't think Dad had a role in it. You know he's in the hospital now? He suffered a stroke." I might as well be shaking my finger at Mickey considering the tone of my rebuke.

Mickey nodded. "You saved Allan, but Becky died."

"Yes, that's the size of it." I reached toward a can of sparkling water but took a Mountain Dew instead, opened it, and took a drink.

Mickey took a Mountain Dew from the drink selections. "Becky decided to take her own life. How tragic. What a thing to see, hear, and smell." She opened her can of pop.

I heard the rush of air from the released carbonation. My breath came quickly. I looked at the fireplace expecting that it had been lit. There was the unmistakable smell of smoke in my nose. I stared at a spot in the chinking between the cabin logs, but it was like I was right back in our pasture.

Mickey guided me through it like she was there too. "It was springtime, almost Easter, wasn't it? Becky gathered sticks and branches she found there in the wooded pasture."

"Yes." I was seeing it all again. I was in my body approaching Becky. I'd ran over the hill from our house, through the trees into the pasture before the big field. The spindly branches of brush tore at my jeans. "I heard Becky before I saw her. She was praying and answering the voice of God, I guess. I've never experienced God the way she described."

"Was she there alone?"

"No. She had Little Man with her." I panted like I'd been running, and my voice sounded strained even to my own ears. "He looked so small. He was so small. He hadn't made a year yet. He was just asleep on a blanket. I didn't know. I thought he was..."

"You thought Little Man might already be dead?"

"Yes." Tears came in torrents.

"It was part of Becky's plan to bring Little Man to the pasture with her. She was planful."

"Becky was always planful." I wiped tears and snot away from my face. "You should have seen her class notes. She was the best student Bend ever had."

"Lorraine, I don't like you talking about this," Becky said. I ignored her right then. It wasn't like it was pleasant for me, either, but this part was my story, my side.

"No one knew where she was. Lorraine, you found her again. You figured it out."

"Our neighbor, Gerry—she's a librarian. Did you know Gerry is Marin's aunt? Gerry knows a lot of things. She told me she'd seen Becky drive her car into the field by the north pasture."

"Lorraine, you knew to ask Gerry if she'd seen Becky. You figured it out. Becky was planful. She gathered sticks. Did she bring the gasoline or did you?"

"Just stop, Lorraine, she can't make you go on," Becky said.

"No, she did. I'd never use gas for a fire in the woods or so close to other trees especially with Allan so near."

"She planned, she gathered sticks, brought gasoline, and a knife. Did she spill the gas accidentally?" Mickey said.

"Hell no, the dumbass did it on purpose—I'm sorry I swore."

"It's okay, Lorraine."

"No, it isn't. It can never be okay." I stared at Mickey begging her to stop me but being unable to stop myself. "I can still see her lift the red metal gas can above her head. Becky was physically strong when she wanted to be. She was weak when it came time to throw hay bales, but she lifted the can above her head and soaked herself in gasoline, her blonde hair, her white dress. Wait, I got that part wrong." I smelled gas and then smoke. "She poured gas on the pile of branches first and then she lit them from stick matches before she soaked herself. We were told to never take those stick matches into the woods. She would be in big trouble if Momma or Dad knew."

"What did Becky do then, Lorraine?"

"She tossed the can aside. Picked up the knife. She stabbed herself and dropped into the fire. How could she do that? How could anyone do that?"

"How by the grace of God could anyone in their right mind do that?" Silence. "If it weren't for you, it could have been Allan on that fire. Just breathe, Lorraine. Becky had wanted to make a sacrifice to God. As I understand it, her first choice was her little boy, but you saved him. I guess she had no other choice but herself."

"Not true." I glared at Mickey and wanted to choke her. "That's not true. Becky had a choice. I told her I'd catch an animal for her. Sheep and goats were acceptable sacrifices in the Bible. I knew from Sunday school. Becky knew it too. We had Holcum's sheep in our pasture. I told her I'd catch one, but she said that wasn't good enough. Momma and Becky always had something to say about what was good enough."

Mickey said, "Becky had a choice. She prepared, planned, and implemented her plan even though she had other options. She seemed quite determined."

"Oh, that's Becky all right. She's stubborn and tough like, I don't know, good grade canvas."

"Yes, like Duluth Trading Store quality canvas."

"I don't know. We probably can't afford it, but Becky was tough."

Micky continued, "No one on her own was going to stop Becky from doing what she was convinced needed to be done."

"You know she probably got pregnant while I was chaperoning her dates with Kenny." My tone stayed angry and I didn't care. "Becky did whatever Becky wanted. Momma and Dad couldn't stop her. Momma wanted me to keep her from getting pregnant so she wouldn't lose the scholarship we both wanted."

"Lorraine, did you let her get pregnant, so you'd get the scholarship?"

"No, Becky and Kenny did that on their own. I couldn't stop them."

"No, you couldn't stop her from getting pregnant and losing that scholarship. It wasn't your job."

"It wasn't my job." Was it my job? I hadn't asked for the job or trained for it. I was just assigned like our family was assigned to monitor Becky after she came out of the hospital.

"What did you do? You brought a helpless child to safety. You were alone with Becky."

"Kenny, Dad, Momma, and Twitch came too late."

"You had to deal with it all by yourself without help from any of the other adults."

"Twitch told me the coroner said Becky didn't suffer. He said the knife wound killed her before she fell in the fire. More bullshit. I can still hear her screams. I'd rather listen to her put me down than hear her screams again." I turned to Mickey. "You want to know what she asked me today?"

"What did Becky say?"

"Just this morning she was yammering on about how she couldn't feel the fire. That's a lie too."

"There's been lies and information withheld all along, hasn't there?" Mickey knew.

"I wish I could have grabbed her, but I didn't get there in time. I needed to get Allan away from the fire, the knife, from her."

"Of course, Lorraine. You did the right thing and only possible thing. Becky still died like she planned. You're angry with her for that. It wasn't your job to save her." Mickey tossed a cloth handkerchief to me. "Sometimes, it doesn't matter what anybody does, how hard anybody tries. People still kill themselves. It's a son of a bitch!"

Becky didn't say anything. I closed my eyes.

Chapter Eleven

So, This Is Therapy

I must have slept. I didn't dream. No dreams makes for better sleep for me. When I awakened, I smelled homemade soup and baked bread. When on earth had Momma found time to make soup and bread? Why on earth would she make soup and bread in summer? My momma would say I can live on canned soup and sandwiches but that doesn't mean I can't appreciate good food. Momma had provided tons of it over the years, and contrary to her ideas, I appreciated good cooking and had learned a thing or two.

I suddenly remembered I wasn't home on the farm. I was in a lake cabin passed out from therapy. I smelled the soup again. I guessed it was bean soup. Great, like there wasn't enough gas in the cabin already. I could distinguish the smells of beans: pinto, navy, and kidney beans softening and comingling with a genuine ham hock and vegetables sautéed a bit before entering the vegetable broth, although it might have been chicken broth. I'd have to ask. Ricky always asked lots of questions when he was around Momma. He asked cooking questions like Momma held the most important secrets of the universe. Maybe, she did.

"You're awake. I thought you might sleep through the evening. It would fit. Talking about trauma is exhausting work. You worked very hard, Lorraine." Mickey brought napkins and soup spoons to a small table. The soup bowls were by the stove. She took a loaf of crusty bread from the oven. I recognized the label—you only had to heat it in its own bag to have something akin to fresh baked bread. I wouldn't mention the shortcut to Momma.

"What time is it?" I stood next to Mickey as she ladled bean soup into bowls. "Your soup smells wonderful."

"I've been working on it much of the day if you count soaking the beans. It's nearly five thirty. I suppose you have a date tonight, a young person like yourself." She took a seat at the small table and blew on her soup.

I joined her. "I should probably call Marin. I want to stop at Ricky and Russ's place to see them, Allan, and Frankie. Ricky and I have to watch out because the farmhands who hurt us might be back in the area." I tucked into the soup, dipping a buttered slice of crusty bread into the savory broth. "This is good."

"Thank you." Mickey stopped eating. "What do you mean you have to watch out?"

"Well, you remember when Ricky Johnson was beat up and left for dead tied to a wooden gate on the County line? Did you live here then?"

"I remember. Awful. He was your friend and you found him."

"Yeah, Dad and I found Ricky after he'd been hurt. Once he was well enough to leave the hospital, Momma, Dad, and I nursed him at our house. Lewis and Petey, two farmhands, came after him to see what he remembered about the beating. They were really rough on both of us."

Mickey left the table but not for long. When she returned, she had an empty baby food jar, the towheaded infant smiling from the label, and a box of jelly beans—the good brand.

"Dessert?" I asked.

"No, therapy. Let me get this straight, Lorraine. In your life you have dealt with being rejected by your momma for being lesbian. Your dad didn't stick up for you with your momma." She took a bean from the box and dropped it in the jar. I nodded. "You lost your scholarship because you were lesbian." She put a bean in the jar. "Your sister went missing and you feared she was murdered by her husband?" She dropped a bean in the jar.

"I like the bean theme you have going on, Mickey, but what does it mean?"

"Think of each of these beans as a trauma in your life—we won't judge one from another in severity. Right now, we are getting a rough estimate of quantity."

"Trauma? Like an act of God or car accident? Next, you're going to tell me I have PTSD. I've heard of it, but I don't know that saying I have it helps anything." I wasn't used to looking at my life this way. I didn't like it.

"Traumas are subjective. We each decide what is a trauma in our own lives and there's no expiration date. You might identify something as a trauma you didn't much consciously think about at the time it happened. You don't have to believe me when I call something a trauma.

"A trauma shakes you, changes you, scares you, stops you or maybe propels you in a new direction. Traumas can leave marks or not. A trauma can be like that little fender bender you were in that didn't leave a dent in your car but God damn it if your neck doesn't ache for the next twenty years.

"We see, feel, smell, taste, and hear traumas in our lives and mostly we keep going like nothing has happened, but our body keeps a tally of what we've been through, done, witnessed happening to others. There's trauma in our bones from the generations before us whether we were the master or the slave, the captor or the captive.

"There are traumas that we agree as a community are permissible to acknowledge and mark or commemorate. Others are shrouded under an expectation of privacy and accepted blame and shame."

"I think I get it. Okay, add a bean for seeing Becky die. Add another for my fear she was going to kill Little Man." I didn't know whether I trusted her system, but I played along. "Finding Ricky was certainly worth a bean." She put another jelly bean in the jar. "Do breakups and disappointments in romance count?"

"Yes, they count."

"We may need a bigger jar. Drop two more in the jar. They can keep company with a bean for Lewis and Petey coming after Ricky and me. Oh, put in a bean for me thinking J.C. McGerber raped his foster child, Addie. She had a miscarriage. Momma, Twitch, and I helped her. Turned out it wasn't J.C. McGerber who got her pregnant. It was her boyfriend, Petey, the cowhand who runs with Lewis."

Plink, plink, plink.

"Add another for Dr. Jacks showing up with an ax to kill Ricky and me. A bean for having to shoot him and another for living with what I did." I stopped myself there. I took a big breath. "Did you know I shot a person? I killed a man. Technically he died of sepsis in the hospital, but the wound he had, I gave him when he was going to bring my dad's splitting ax down on Ricky and me." I swallowed hard.

"I shot Dr. Jacks in the shoulder. Ricky and I crawled out from under that man's bleeding body and drove into town not sure who I'd shot and whether he was the last of those who were after us. If he hadn't been a doctor, he would have bled out in our living room. He knew how to stop the bleeding enough for him to live until the ambulance came. The asshole never admitted who put him up to coming after us, but I know who did it."

Plink. Plink.

"Add a bean for thinking I'd killed Warren McGerber and telling his brother I did. Add one for him showing up alive. A bean for knowing what Warren

McGerber did and not being able to prove it. A bean for telling Charity that I couldn't be her girlfriend if she were going to travel in Europe with Kelly. I guess a bean for leaving home for vet school even though it was my dream. It was frightening. It changed me."

Mickey lifted the jar and shook it. The beans rattled against one another and the glass, sounding like coins.

"Are you trying to tell me I'm full of beans, Mickey?" I gave a faint laugh.

"Yes, Lorraine Tyler, you're full of beans all right. I'm trying to tell you it's too early to assume you have a major mental illness. You've experienced so many traumas. And it makes sense you hear your sister's voice. Like it or not she was a measuring stick of what was right and good. I suspect there's more for you two to argue about and negotiate."

I looked at the clock on my phone. "I need to get going. I want to stop at Ricky and Russ's and check on Frankie." I hoped she hadn't tied up Justin and stuffed him in her suitcase—no, he was too big to fit, but she might just tie him up and put him in the bed of my truck to bring back to Duluth with her. I wanted to see Little Man—Allan. A shower and change of clothes seemed like a good idea. "I want to stop at the hospital and see Dad. I should call Marin and Charity, too, I suppose." I wiped my mouth and moved away from the table.

"You mentioned being a twin. It got me thinking about how different you look from Becky."

"Yep. I always say that in Biblical terms, Becky and I were the Jacob and Esau of Bend. I was the hairy firstborn, fixated on animals, born every bit as dark as Becky was light. Like the twins of the Old Testament story, we competed since we were in the womb, and like the twins of the Old Testament, Momma favored the younger one. You know that Twitch is our dad and obviously we aren't identical."

Mickey didn't say anything. She just looked at me. I wondered what she was thinking.

I scanned the room as though I may have brought things with me when I came. I had no belongings there and if anything, I was leaving with less than what I came with. I waved goodbye.

"Be careful, Lorraine. Come back to see me tomorrow." Mickey stood by Tumor in the open door of the cabin. I supposed she worried I'd use up her whole box of jelly beans.

Chapter Twelve

Old Friends

On my way to Russ's place my cell phone rang again. I know I'm not supposed to use a cell phone and drive, but I answered anyway. I lived dangerously. I'd been to therapy. There was silence on the other end. After having said all those things to Mickey I guess I was emboldened.

"Hey, you asshole. If you're calling me, I'm guessing you want to talk. So, talk! If you're planning to kill me to keep me from being a witness against you this is a piss-poor sneak attack. Besides, I want Warren McGerber punished. I don't care about you." They didn't hang up.

"Goddammit, Lorraine. You never let up."

It was Lewis.

"You're the one calling me," I said. My heart was thumping in my chest, but I kept my voice level. "What do you want?" I pulled to the side of the road, parked, and killed the engine.

"I want to come home," he said.

Charity had called Bend home and now Lewis called Bend home. "What's keeping you from coming home?" Like I didn't know. "I heard you were already in the area."

"You know very well what's keeping me away. That asshole McGerber didn't pay me the money he promised to Petey and me. We planned to put a down payment on our own place. Now, because we listened to that nut, we're wanted men."

I wanted to tell the fool he was a wanted man because he held Ricky and me captive and had threatened to hurt me if I didn't remove Ricky's jaw wires with Lewis's dirty, rusty wire cutters. McGerber got them to do his nastiness for him. Those were the reasons why Lewis and Petey were wanted men. That's what I wanted to say, but I didn't. If I bitched him out too much, I wouldn't know where to find him.

"What do you want, Lewis?"

"I want to meet with you face-to-face and talk."

Where does this land on the list of bad ideas?

"How do I know you aren't planning to kill me and get rid of one of the witnesses against you? I heard you tried to run Ricky off the road."

"What? I never did. I saw him and tried to catch up to him to apologize, but he drove crazy. I didn't follow him into his yard. I didn't trust he wouldn't ram me. I figured I'd spooked him so bad. That's why I've been calling you too."

"Where are you now?"

Silence.

"Where are you, Lewis?"

"I'm parked about a hundred yards behind you."

Shit. I looked in my rearview mirror. A dark-green pickup truck was on the shoulder of the road just like me. I hadn't noticed. "I'm not meeting with you unless it's some place kind of public."

"That's fine. I've been waiting for you to finish up with that therapist woman. Nancy?"

"You know about Nancy? She's calling herself Mickey now."

"Yeah, that sounds about right. She still got that farty dog?"

It was surreal talking about my therapist with Lewis. "Yes, Tumor is alive and farting." *Probably not for long.* "What should we do next?"

"Meet me at the Lake Tavern parking lot. It's public. Please hear me out in person. You can trust that I'm not planning to kill you anymore than you're planning to have the sheriff waiting to arrest me."

There was silence on the line. I suppose we were both weighing how much we trusted each other.

"Come on, Lorraine. We cut the horns off a killer bull together. Shouldn't us both working a farm mean something?"

Asshole. It was unfair to invoke the sacred labors of underappreciated ranch hands and apprentice veterinarians. It should mean something that we'd had each other's back that day working J.C. McGerber's farm, but I didn't know if it meant enough. Still, Lewis and Petey were my best chance at getting Warren McGerber charged with Ricky's beating. "What time do you want to meet?"

"How about now?"

"I guess now is good."

*

He drove by in his big truck. He could have easily rammed the side of my small truck and killed me, but he didn't. I don't know why him sparing me then made me trust him, but I followed him to the Lake Tavern.

During the drive I thought of the people I should have told about my planned meeting with Lewis but didn't. Too late. I pulled into the Lake Tavern parking lot. Besides, it's illegal to use a cell phone while driving.

It was still light out. Lewis parked under the trees at the back of the parking lot by the dumpsters. He was sitting on the tailgate drinking a beer by the time I parked my truck closer to the building amongst the rows of cars and trucks near the front door of the Tavern.

Lewis had probably brought his beer with him. I think most days he kept a cooler of cold Coors Beer in the back of his truck. I doubted he'd risk entering the tavern. Someone might call the sheriff on him—not that there was a reward, but people like fireworks and another's misery is its own type of entertainment.

I scanned the cab of my truck for a weapon of self-defense. The dusty, plastic ice scraper from the glove box would have to do. As I approached him, I searched his face for an indication of his true intentions. I scanned his clothes and the area for weapons. I didn't see any weapons, but he could have something in his pockets or the waistband of his jeans.

"Hello, Lorraine. Would you like a beer?"

"No, thanks." I walked closer. He scooted over like he was making room for me to sit beside him on the truck tailgate. It was both familiar and weird as shit.

"I didn't know if you'd come," he said as I sat beside him. "I thought you might hightail it in the opposite direction once I told you I was following you." He pushed his cowboy hat back on his head.

"I admit it creeped me out. I wasn't so sure I would come here either. Then I pictured parking my truck on your chest and the truck just drove here on autopilot." I swung my legs from the tailgate. My feet didn't reach the gravel of the parking lot surface.

"Park on my chest? That ain't who you are, Lorraine." Lewis crushed his empty can and threw it into the open recycling bin beside the tavern dumpster.

"Who are you, Lewis?" I asked.

"Good question," Lewis said. "I always thought I knew. You know Warren McGerber is a slick bastard."

"Is this where you make excuses for what you did?" I asked.

"No, but I would like you to understand how it came to be. Nobody or at least not very many people get up in the morning and think, 'Today, I'm going to do something heinous for money. I'm going to bully two friends, scare them, and threaten them further harm if they don't cooperate with what I want, which isn't even what I want, it's what some other guy wants, and he has the money to buy what he wants. And I want his money. I want his money so goddamned much that I will believe every piece of shit comes out his mouth." Lewis brushed some dust off the leg of his jeans. "God, it sounds like bad cable TV."

"I get it Lewis." *I didn't really.* "McGerber's promise of money tempted you and Petey."

The next prattle made me want to vomit, but I needed to get Lewis to snitch on McGerber and he wasn't going to get there by me haranguing him. He was an entitled white man. "You've worked hard on farms all over Minnesota. You've done the strenuous, dirty labor that put money and time in other farmers' and ranchers' accounts. You want to work for yourself." I punched him in the arm, not so hard he would need to hit me back, but with some force.

"I still hate you for what you did." Understatement of the year. "You said some really shitty things to me, and you gave Ricky and me both some new nightmares like we didn't have enough of those. I'm really pissed off at you and Petey. Don't even get me started on Petey having a sexual relationship with Addie." I hit him again. It wasn't enough, but I didn't know there could ever be enough hurting him to make up for what I felt. I had the slightest hope he was sorry enough to help get McGerber, then maybe I could find my way to forgive him or at least not actively imagine driving over both Lewis and Petey with my truck.

He rubbed his arm but stayed seated on the truck. "That's fair. I don't think I'd believe you if you said you weren't pissed. Just so you know, Petey loves Addie. I think she cares for him too. It's a romance. You may have heard, we can't help who we love."

Lewis turned to face me. We sat close. I noticed his eyes were green and there was a hint of red in his full beard. He smelled like cigarettes, beer, and mint gum. "I want to apologize to you and to Ricky if he'll let me."

He choked a bit on the words. Apologizing was not a familiar activity. It wasn't for me either. I didn't say anything, never one to make amends easy for others. I suspected he had more to say.

"I was hoping you would…ah shit. I don't know what I was thinking." Lewis pushed off the tailgate and put his hands in his pockets as he paced and looked into the sky.

"Just say what you came to say, Lewis. I haven't got all day. I have things to do."

"More therapy?"

"Not until tomorrow. You may have heard I've had what people who make more money than you or me call a traumatic life. Talking about it is supposed to help."

"Hmm, I suppose that makes some sense if you aren't a good forgetter or like to drink a lot. I knew you saw your sister burn up."

"Yeah, I did."

He sat again on the truck. His legs were long enough that his feet reached the dirt. He kicked in the gravel with his cowboy boot. "Did I add to your nightmares?"

"Yeah. I've been scared you would come after Ricky or me again." My voice cracked as I began to cry.

"I won't. I promise. I'm sorry. I shouldn't have done anything like that to anyone and I will never do something like that again. All I've ever wanted in my life is a piece of land to farm—have a few cattle, maybe sheep and goats, some chickens. I could live the rest of my days just tending that place."

I wiped away my tears and snot. "I hope you get it, Lewis." I meant what I said even if I still hated him.

"Lorraine, would you talk to the sheriff or the court on our behalf? Maybe Petey and I could both start over. We'd do restitution or some shit like that—whatever it took."

How long had I waited for this moment? "Hell, yes. I'll talk to anybody you want. Give me a list. You testify against Warren McGerber..."

Lewis stood up and slapped his cowboy hat against the side of his leg. I stood too. I faced him.

He shook his head side to side. "Oh Christ, testify against Warren McGerber? I didn't say anything about testifying."

I remembered when Lewis, Petey, and I had worked together on Warren's brother J.C.'s farm. Lewis saw when Twitch slugged J.C. McGerber because he had asked me to dehorn his maniac bull, Killer. Twitch was really angry

McGerber had purposely endangered me. McGerber yelled at Petey and Lewis that they were witnesses of Twitch's assault. Lewis had said, "I'm a spectator, never a witness." I guess his edict held true today.

"Warren McGerber is a dangerous man," Lewis continued, shaking his head at the idea of testifying against him.

"No shit, you don't have to convince me. He's a dangerous man who almost beat Ricky to death."

"Here's the thing. I didn't think he beat Ricky because of the way he doted on Ricky at the Lake Tavern. Warren flirted with Ricky. I never believed he would beat him or get any others to do it."

I couldn't believe what I was hearing, and I couldn't believe Lewis believed what he was saying.

He kept talking, "When he hired Petey and me to find out what Ricky remembered I didn't know Warren was protecting himself. He said God had sent angels to deliver a judgment from Him and we were to get a preview of the miracle Ricky witnessed."

I rolled my eyes and wanted to smack Lewis in the head. "Are you listening to yourself? Don't you hear the madness in the line of bull Warren McGerber sold to you? Were you so enamored with his money you lost your whole brain?"

"Why would Warren flirt with Ricky if he hated queers so much?" Lewis looked honestly flummoxed.

"I don't know. I can guess." Oh, I knew. Especially after Warren had as much as bragged today at the gas station about having raped Ricky. "It could be Warren McGerber is attracted to men himself. He might have been willing to be sexual with Ricky if he knew he wouldn't get caught." I didn't even want to think about all the things that may have happened to Ricky that night. "Maybe Warren McGerber hated his own homosexual impulses and felt like he was atoning for his feelings by beating up Ricky. I don't know and I don't care. He's dangerous and he will be even more dangerous if he is elected to congress."

"I don't know who's going to beat him. The other candidate has three strikes against her. She's a woman, she's Black, and I heard she's Muslim. I don't know why they're bothering with an election."

"Are you serious?" I thought he had already said the dumbest thing he could.

"Yes, I'm serious. No one around here is going to vote for a terrorist." Despite his agitation Lewis sat down on the truck next to me again.

"I don't know about her religion but being Muslim doesn't make her a terrorist. Islam doesn't support terrorism any more than Christianity does. It's the extremists who want to make their religion an excuse to oppress and kill others. I will not blame that on God."

"My, my haven't you gotten all spiritual. You forgotten how the church feels about queers?"

"I've always been spiritual just not always perfectly religious. And no, I haven't forgotten what some people think they need to hate in order to follow their religions.

Back to Warren McGerber, he can't win a campaign if he can't run. He can't run if he is in jail for a hate crime."

"Who is going to believe my or Petey's word against Warren McGerber?" His words hung in the air despite how heavy they were. "Add to that, we ran. That makes us look guilty as hell. Dr. Jacks is dead and can't back us up even if he would have told the truth. Last I heard, Ricky doesn't remember what happened the night of the beating. Did he get his memory back?"

I shook my head.

"Even if he did, we'd just have the word of two queers and a couple of ranch hands."

I wanted to argue with him but part of me knew he was right, and he had a lot to risk turning himself in and he wasn't truly ready to risk it. I didn't know how I could possibly help Lewis have the moral transformation that would allow him to see the necessity of being truly sorry and taking the responsibility of suffering the consequences of acting so hateful. I was just an almost vet not a therapist, priest, or probation officer. I took a different approach. "I suppose we are just going to have to get that asshole to confess."

Chapter Thirteen

Trust Me, I've Seen it Work on TV

Lewis and I conspired. Well, I told Lewis my plan and he fought me on it, but he didn't kill me or drive away. Progress, not perfection.

"Get a message to Warren that you want to meet him. Tell him you want your money or you're going to talk to the sheriff." I felt on fire like every crime show I'd ever seen was at the disposal of my big brain. I even employed hand gestures. "You'll meet him. If he asks about your phone during the meeting, you'll reluctantly give it to him." I paced as I set the scene. "What he won't know is that you have a second phone with a line open transmitting the whole conversation to me. I will be recording the confession you extract."

"And say I agree to meet with Warren, which I haven't. Just how am I supposed to extract that confession?"

Doesn't Lewis watch any television?

"Just ask for your money and let him talk. You should have seen him today when he knew only I could hear him. He wants to gloat about what he'd gotten away with. He thinks he's untouchable."

"What if he doesn't brag to me?"

"I don't know. Ask him genuine questions. If you phrase the question right, he can't help but confess. It's like when you ask somebody, 'have you stopped cheating on your wife?' If the person says yes, they're admitting they used to cheat. If they say no, they're admitting they haven't stopped cheating yet."

I looked at Lewis for any sign he understood me at all. "Ask him if he feels at all bad for beating Ricky? What's he got against him? Say you thought he liked Ricky. That should get him going. Another thing, Warren loves to preach. He loves listening to the sound of his own voice even more than Pastor Grind. But you got to get him to say what he did to Ricky."

"Where should I meet him?" Lewis asked.

The answer came to me in a flash of genius and symmetry. "Tell him to meet you at the approach where he tied up and beat Ricky. I'll come from Kenny's old farm across that big field. I'll hide in the long grasses. Momma has night goggles. He'll just see your truck parked there. He'll be less suspicious."

"Where am I supposed to get this other phone?"

"I'll take care of that. Momma bought one for Dad, but he won't touch the thing."

"How is your dad? I heard he was in the hospital."

"Shit, I need to get to the hospital yet tonight. I'll get you Dad's phone. You get it charged up for the meeting. Hide it in your shirt pocket." *Lorraine Tyler setting up a sting operation.* I was so sure of myself, my plan. I had this manic energy and confidence. "Call him now. He's probably at his brother's place. I'm ashamed to say I still have J.C. McGerber's landline on my contacts list."

"I got Warren's number." Lewis scrolled through his phone.

"Oh." That surprised me. "I suppose you had reason to talk with one another back in the day when he was offering you money for your help." I sounded like a jealous girlfriend, but I didn't want my anger to sabotage my plans for Lewis helping me get McGerber. My stomach turned sour thinking of them conspiring together about Ricky and me. For the first time that evening I doubted my idea, myself.

"Warren?" Lewis had McGerber on the phone. He glanced at me. "I think you know who this is. Yeah, that's right."

I could only hear Lewis's side of the conversation, but it wasn't hard to follow. Lewis did a good job almost like he'd done this sort of subterfuge before, which he had. He'd fooled me into meeting him at our farm when he and Petey came after Ricky and me.

"I think you know damn well why I'm calling. I want my money. We need to meet and settle accounts. No, I'm the boss of this little rendezvous. You don't even have a vote."

I trembled. His tone was the same as when he had Ricky and me captive and reminded me he was the boss and I didn't know as much as I thought I did.

Lewis bossed McGerber on the phone. "Don't worry, you know the spot. Meet me at the approach by the County line. You know, where you done Ricky."

I wanted to vomit at those words—*done Ricky*.

"No, eight tomorrow night, bring the money and come alone. You want to get this business handled. You got your big town hall meeting against your competitor coming up. From what I hear, whichever way Bend votes so goes the district. You don't want anything getting in the way of you making a big splash at that town hall meeting. You don't want to lose to her, do you?" He disconnected the phone and nodded to me. "Tomorrow night, at eight."

"Follow me to our farm. I'll get you another phone."

Chapter Fourteen

Naked Among Friends

I pulled into Ricky and Russ's place later than I'd planned. At this rate I wasn't going to get back to the hospital before visiting hours ended. Shit. All that fooling around at therapy would make me miss seeing Dad before he was asleep. I trusted that Momma and Twitch were with him. Besides, he'd understand why I needed to do what I was doing.

Kenny and Ramona appeared to be leaving. Kenny was carrying Allan, but it was Ramona who had the boy's rapt attention. "Now, I want you to be good for Uncle Ricky and Uncle Russ."

Becky gasped watching the family scene.

"Be good for Russ and Ricky. Ignore flakey Frankie," Kenny added. "Momma Ramona and I will be home in time to read to you and tuck you into bed." Kenny kissed him. Ramona kissed him. "Love you, Allan," Kenny said. Kenny lowered Allan to the ground where he stood in jeans and a tiny pearl snapped western shirt like his daddy wore.

"Love you more," Allan said.

"Love you to the moon and back, my darling," Ramona said.

"Love you more," Allan said as he hugged Ramona's legs.

Becky said quietly, like I wasn't even sure it was her, "He's going to be all right. They're a family. They love each other and they're a family."

I didn't answer. She didn't need my affirmation. I got out of the truck. Waved at Kenny and Ramona. I hauled my duffel bag to the porch where Ricky held Allan's hand as he watched Kenny and Ramona leave on a date.

"It's about time you got here," Ricky said. "We're having ice cream for dinner and we are all making posters to get Allison Jackson elected. Frankie is texting and chatting with all her contacts." He turned and went back in the house.

Frankie was there, all made up and looking every bit as beautiful as she felt inside. She busily thumbed her phone. She, Russ's mom Ruth, Allan, and Justin were in the kitchen making ice cream cones and sundaes. The kitchen table and every other available surface had posters drying. Some were as simple as "Vote for Allison Jackson." Others were more pointed, "A vote for McGerber is a vote for Satan." I suspected Frankie had made the finely illustrated one that said, "Bigots have no balls!"

Allan was clueless but laughing and the rest of them doubled over in fits of laughter. For a moment I forgot about everything in my life but good friends and the promise of fresh vanilla ice cream and political discourse.

"We are babysitting," Ricky hugged me. "You smell bad."

"I know. Can I use your shower?" I headed to the bathroom off the room Ricky shared with Russ with a second door connecting it to Ruth's room. "I've got a lot to tell you after I get cleaned up. I met with Lewis."

A stampede of boots echoed in the hallway. As I was removing my boots and socks, Frankie, Ricky, Russ, Allan, and Justin entered the bedroom. "I'm going to need a little privacy."

"We don't care about your body, Lorraine," Ricky said.

Frankie jumped in, "We care about your body but not sexually. Seeing you naked doesn't arouse us. Actually, it would probably evoke pity."

"Thanks. I still don't plan to be naked in front of you. I just met Justin."

"He played Division One football before he blew out his knee. He's seen bodies way hotter than yours everyday—men and women," Frankie said.

I didn't know how that was supposed to help.

"I think they're anxious, we're all anxious to hear what happened when you met with Lewis," Russ said. "We'll close our eyes, but you better tell us everything."

"All right." This was stranger than usual. I wondered if it warranted a bean in my trauma jar and then decided it didn't. They were my friends and wanted to know what was going on because it affected them too. It wasn't about using me for amusement or arousal. "The hang-up calls have been from Lewis. He called again. It was Lewis you saw. He denies that he was trying to run you off the road."

"What does he want?" Ricky asked, opening one eye.

I sighed. "He says he wants to apologize."

"Did you tell him to go..." Frankie looked down at Allan. "Did you tell him to go fornicate with himself?"

I pulled off my T-shirt. "I called him some names but agreed to meet with him at the Lake Tavern. Once we were there, I punched him a few times."

"What?" They all opened their eyes.

I looked at Frankie. She had told me on a number of occasions that she wanted bigger breasts than I had. "Lewis said he was sorry, and he'd never do something so hateful again."

The four voluntarily blinded spectators mumbled and grumbled. They probably knew how often promises of no violence were broken.

"Who's Lewis?" Allan asked.

"He should be sorry," Ricky said.

"He should be hung up by his balls," Russ said.

"Hey, now let Lorraine finish. No talking disparagingly about balls," Frankie said.

Justin put his arm around Frankie's shoulder and pulled her close. *He knows about Frankie's transition.* I wanted to pull Frankie off to the side and ask her what happened. Did she attack Justin or just talk to him? I'd have to wait for the story from Frankie.

"Allan, honey, Lewis is a man who did some dumb things and he's sorry for doing them now." I peeled off my jeans. I was down to my underpants and bra. No one laughed. I wondered if Ricky would peek and then hassle me that I didn't wax. Ah, screw it. I took off my underclothes and went into the bathroom. They followed, bumping into one another with their eyes closed. I pulled the shower curtain back and started the shower. I put my hand in the stream of water waiting for the right temperature, but my own modesty encouraged me to get under the cold stream of water. I pulled the shower curtain closed.

"I convinced Lewis to call Warren McGerber and set up a meeting to get his money. McGerber fell for it. We're meeting him at the approach..."

I heard Ricky gasp. "It's okay," Russ said. I imagined Russ hugged Ricky.

I stayed under the stream of water. Finally, it warmed up. It had been so cold I suspected my nipples could cut glass. I would have to remember to tell Charity that one. I could still hear Ricky sobbing. I didn't want to think of the traumas Ricky still felt every day. He was full of beans too.

"We're meeting him tomorrow night. We're going to record him admitting to hurting you, Ricky. We're going to get him."

"Get him," Allan said.

"You make it sound so easy. Do you think he will just admit it?" Frankie asked.

"Maybe he'll pay Lewis. Either way we are going to get him. I'm going to hide in the middle of Hollister field straight out from the approach. I'll have my phone with an open line to the phone Lewis has hidden. We'll catch and record Warren's confession."

"I should go with you," Ricky said.

A chorus of voices saying no followed.

"No, I can do this. Then we won't have to worry about Warren McGerber being in government or coming after us or anyone else again."

"Being a lone wolf again, Lorraine?" Frankie said. "I don't know. It sounds like this guy could twist anything to make him look like a better candidate."

I turned off the shower and pulled back the curtain. They all stood there staring at me and then were suddenly embarrassed that they had forgotten to keep their eyes closed and rushed from the bathroom, closing the door as they fled.

"Thanks, your reaction to my nude body gives me a lot of confidence." I got out of the shower and began toweling off. "Anyway," I called out into the other room expecting that they were at least still listening to me, "don't call me on my cell the next couple hours. I'm going to visit Dad. Tomorrow night, I'm going to sting Warren McGerber. Soon this nightmare will all be over." I looked at the clock on my phone. "Shit, I got to see my dad."

"I saw him this afternoon," Ricky said. "He's still pretty tired. Twitch and Peggy are with him."

I came out into the bedroom. Frankie had laid out some clothes from my duffel bag.

"Ricky, I thought you weren't supposed to return to the hospital without permission from nursing."

"I snuck in. I don't like being told where I can and cannot go. I love your momma and dad. I wanted to see them. Besides, I couldn't leave him without some product in his hair. It would ruin my reputation."

"Thanks, Ricky." I dressed, corralled my wet hair under a baseball hat, and checked the time. "I've got to go. Wish me luck."

Allan hugged my legs. "Good luck, Raine."

Chapter Fifteen

After Visiting Hours

It was technically after visiting hours. I had a speech all prepared if any nurse or doctor tried to stop me from seeing my dad, but no one did. Instead, they gave me pitying looks which scared me more than Warren McGerber. Nurse Faison came up close. She must have been pulling a double shift. "Your dad had a turn. He's got a lot of chest congestion gathering strength to become pneumonia."

Oh God, no.

Hospital acquired pneumonia was often hard to treat because the bacteria causing it may be resistant to antibiotics and because Dad was already sick. I tried to sound nonplused. "Yeah, Dad'll tell you he's smoked since he was five years old and it doesn't hurt you none. He brags about it. No surprise that his lungs are wet and weak. Does he have a fever?"

"We're giving him IV antibiotics and his fever is down." Nurse Faison looked over toward Dad's room.

I hazarded more questions trying to show I wasn't a medical idiot. "How's his oxygen levels?"

"Within normal limits."

"Oximeter or blood gases?"

She smiled at me. "Both."

"I asked because…"

"You're asking because you love your dad and you know although oximetry reading is noninvasive, it's peripheral and not as accurate as arterial oxygen saturation which is determined through the analysis of blood gases." She looked me in the eye. "You love your dad, and you may not be able to control his illness but you can use your medical knowledge to ask questions and make sure we're doing our job."

"I didn't mean to suggest you weren't doing your job," I said.

"I know. There are so few things within our control when a loved one is sick. We keep watch on what we can. Let me know if you have more questions." She started to walk away, but turned back and said, "Stay as long as you want. There's a second recliner in there. Just don't let your momma rile him up."

"Then I'll work on global warming and if there's time, I'll try to sort out a peace accord in the Middle East. Wish me luck." I was needing lots of luck.

She laughed and returned to the nurse's desk.

Momma was of course sitting next to Dad's bed and talking at him. I took a deep breath and went into the room.

"Where have you been, Lorraine? I suppose you were busy with Marin or Charity or whichever girl you're kissing these days." Momma looked more worried than mad.

"Yep, sounds like me." I didn't argue with her. Let her think what she wanted. Dad was asleep. He had oxygen on which was an addition from when I'd seen him earlier in the day.

"How is he?"

"Asleep. He has pneumonia. Smoking is the devil's work."

"Pneumonia is always a risk in the hospital," I said. It seemed like the least awful thing to say.

"Is Ricky home?" Momma asked.

I didn't know if she was confused at first. Maybe she was thinking about when he used to live with us at the farm so I'd know where he was. "He's at home with Russ and Frankie. Kenny and Ramona are on a date. Allan is having ice cream with Ruth, Ricky, and Frankie." I didn't mention Frankie's posters or Justin. "Momma, I'm worried that Warren McGerber will be elected a senator."

"Oh, a fool like him won't win the election." She said it as confidently as if I'd suggested having nominated the Easter Bunny.

"What makes you so sure, Momma?"

"Times are changing. I think Bend is going to vote for the nice Black lady. As Bend goes, so goes the district. You don't like me saying but God will find a way to make it right."

I took the chair on the other side of Dad's bed and lowered my head onto his leg just above the knee.

Becky said, "You better stay awake with Dad, Lorraine."

I ignored Becky. Momma had spoken. God would make it right.

Chapter Sixteen

Morning Has Broken

When I awakened Dad was talking with Twitch. Momma had stepped out of the room or maybe she'd been kicked out, I didn't know. I was just so relieved to see Dad alert, awake, and alive.

"Dad, how do you feel?"

"About what I expect death warmed over feels like. I keep expecting to find a cow is sitting on my chest every time I try to take a big breath, but they say I'm getting better. I might get out on Saturday."

"I'm so glad. I was worried about you." I took his hand. There were so many things I wanted to tell him. So many things I knew couldn't be his worry right now, but I was used to telling him.

"You never have to worry about me. I'm always just where and how I'm supposed to be." He smiled. His brown eyes looked like pools of chocolate but had a sparkle anyway. "Hitch your wagon to this guy if you want to go somewhere different." He tilted his head toward Twitch. Twitch blushed. I wondered if Dad was a little wonky from the meds or lack of oxygen. Sometimes the steroids make a person manic.

"Out, out, we've all got to be out. Nurse Faison has some procedures and tests to run and she doesn't need us under her feet." Momma waved her arms like she was directing traffic at a busy intersection.

Wow, Momma was singing a new tune, getting the rest of us in line to follow another nurse's orders. No one argued. "I'll see you later, Dad."

"Go to the town hall." He coughed. Caught his breath. "Cheer at everything Mrs. Jackson does. I don't care if she farts or sneezes, you cheer," Dad said.

"I will. I heard you made that town hall meeting possible. Thank you, Dad."

"Yeah, yeah." He choked up again, not just his breathing but for being acknowledged for having done something brave and generous.

"Why didn't you tell me you were going to PFLAG?" He waved me off like I'd said too much. I guessed he was embarrassed by the attention or Momma hearing. I didn't tell Momma or Dad that I'd met with Lewis or the scheme we had made. I didn't want to be talked out of it and I didn't want anybody taking control over it or being injured by it.

Twitch followed me out. "McGerber going to be a senator?"

"Looks like it." I didn't tell Twitch about my plan with Lewis either. He would have been the logical helper. Momma could stay with Dad, but it just seemed like Twitch needed to be with them now, too, not following me in my sting operation.

"Momma said we should trust God to make it right."

Twitch nodded. He didn't dispute the sentiment and neither did I. Then he walked away down the hallway stopping to talk to the young nurse who had flirted with him the day before.

I had slept through the night in my dad's hospital room. Initially, I'd been leaning against his leg, but some kind soul must have tucked me back in the recliner they'd added on my side of the bed earlier in the day. The good soul had covered me with a blanket. Maybe it was Momma who did it. The kindness saved me a stiff neck and helped me catch up on some of my missing sleep. When I was fully awake, I remembered that Marin had expected me at her place last night and Mickey had told me to come back to her cabin this morning for another therapy session and then we would see where we were and make a plan.

"Wasn't one trip to the witch doctor enough, Lorraine?" Becky said.

*

I drove to the lake. On the way I tried to call Ricky, but he didn't pick up and I didn't leave a message. I thought about calling Frankie but that conversation was going to take some time and needed to happen in person so I had the full benefit of Frankie's telling.

I'd missed about a hundred calls from Marin and another hundred texts. I scrolled through the texts quickly. The gist of it was that she had to go to the girls' ranch to calm Addie who was afraid of Petey getting arrested. I didn't call her back then. I'd do my therapy and then worry about my love life.

It took less time to drive along the winding road to Mickey's cabin for my second therapy session. I was aware I felt less nervous about it. I wasn't ready to say I was looking forward to talking to her. I saw the red fox again like it had waited for me to come by and get a glimpse before it disappeared back into the woods.

Mickey was sitting in a bright-green Adirondack chair out front of her cabin. The summer morning was still cool, she wore a jeans jacket and a wool cap. She waved me into the cabin. We sat at the little wooden table.

"Well, you're alive and you look like you might have slept some if your hair is any indication."

"My hair always looks like I've been sleeping or in a wind tunnel." I ran my hands over my curls and took the baseball cap from my back pocket and put it on.

"What's happened since I last saw you? How many beans do we need to add to your jar or can we take some out? How's your dad?"

"Pneumonia. I slept in his room last night. He was awake this morning—maybe a little wonky."

"What do you mean wonky?"

"I don't know. He said something about me hitching my wagon to Twitch if I want to get somewhere."

"I take it your dad knows you know Twitch is your biological father, right?" Mickey asked.

"Yes, he knows. He wouldn't likely forget it. I told you what happened, didn't I? You're going to love this. Get a jar and some jelly beans out for my momma's life. When Momma was seventeen or eighteen her little brother suffocated in the grain bin while she was in charge of watching him. Can you imagine how you'd feel?"

"Yes, I have an idea." Mickey added another bean to the jar.

"Hey, what're you doing? That was Momma's trauma."

"Trust me, it spills over. Go ahead, tell me the rest."

"Well, Momma's parents, particularly her dad blamed her for her little brother William's death. In fact, Grandpa went so far as to accuse Momma of whoring with Allister Grind, whom we now know as Pastor Grind, when she was supposed to be watching William. Momma was devastated by this false accusation especially coming from her parents. She left home before graduation and didn't tell them where she was going. That's how she came to Bend. She'd run away from home, no money, no diploma. She got a job at Will's Diner and met Twitch and got pregnant. Then she met my dad and fell in love and married him."

Mickey's forehead wrinkled like a shar-pei. "Mmmm, interesting."

"What?" I helped myself to the chocolate chip banana muffin she slid on a plate to me. She'd cut it in half and smeared it with butter.

"I was just thinking last night about twins. Do you think it's possible that you and Becky had different fathers?" Mickey bit into a muffin.

"What? From each other? That's kind of crazy sounding even for you, no offense." I bit into the muffin and thought about what she'd asked.

Mickey asked me, "Can a woman release more than one egg during ovulation?"

"Yes, that's how you get fraternal twins. Two eggs are fertilized as opposed to one egg fertilized and then splitting."

"What if a woman releases more than one egg during a time period when she has sex with more than one man? Could two eggs be fertilized but by different men?" Mickey's eyes widened as she looked at me.

We both pulled out our phones and pecked away. Googling by the lake during therapy.

"Shit."

"Superfecundation."

"Shit."

"Okay, say your momma came to Bend during the time of her fertile window."

"Fertile window? Was that a Hitchcock movie?" I joked not quite ready to wrap my head around what Mickey was suggesting.

She smiled briefly. "You're a vet. I assume you know what a fertile window is?"

"Yes, I know. It's the time period during a woman's menstrual cycle when pregnancy is possible. It is the couple days before ovulation and once ovulation occurs the egg remains viable for twelve to forty-eight hours before it begins to disintegrate."

"How long can sperm live?"

"Three days."

"So? Would it be accurate to say that the fertile span could last maybe, theoretically five to seven days?"

"I suppose, theoretically, but the conditions would have to be right or even plotted." Oh God, Mickey was fearless. My momma would want to strangle the woman for even thinking what she was about to say to me.

"What if your momma met Joseph and knew he was the love of her life, but she got scared that she might be pregnant from having sex with Twitch? What would she do?"

That hussy.

Becky said, "Leave now, Lorraine. Don't listen to this."

I shrugged.

"So, she had to hope she wasn't pregnant or..."

"Or she... God, I don't think I can say it. She'll know. She'll know and materialize right here at this cabin and whack me with her New Testament."

"Peggy, your momma meets Joseph. She is immediately smitten with him. She thinks about her encounter with Twitch which may have been a knee-jerk reaction to her parents having already accused her of being a loose woman."

I interrupted, "Not just that. Twitch is very handsome and charming. He has a reputation for seducing many women, married or not."

Becky said, "Twitch is a man whore."

"I assume your mother wasn't on birth control. Birth control wasn't very available or popular."

"And carrying a condom is more a recent habit for Twitch."

"Yes, from what you've said, he's charming. Peggy was young, vulnerable, traumatized, alone in a new place. She meets a charming man at her new job. Against her better judgment she is sexual for the first time ever with this handsome stranger. Then, a day or two later she meets Joseph. Joseph is everything her heart has desired. She thinks, 'But what if it will all be spoiled by my ending up pregnant with this other man's child?' What would she do?"

I let the idea swim around in my head as I started a second muffin and got myself a glass of milk from Mickey's refrigerator. Therapy was different than I had expected.

"So, you think it's possible my momma decided to be sexual with Joseph, too, to keep it within the realm of possibility that if she was pregnant, he'd accept that the baby, in this case twins, belonged to him?"

"I don't know anything for certain and neither would you without DNA testing, but I was playing in my mind thinking of all the scenarios that might make sense. I don't know your momma. Maybe she's not even capable of such planning, scheming, and self-preservation."

"Oh, she's capable, but I'm sure as hell not asking Momma if she had sex with Dad, too, her first couple days in Bend."

"No, I don't suppose you'd want to ask her such a thing. Even if it's true, it's not about being bad. It's about surviving."

"I'm not asking Dad either. This is crazy talk."

"Just spitballing here, Lorraine. It's all speculation."

"If Momma created the possibility that Dad was our biological father, why would she tell him we were Twitch's?"

"That's a good question. Maybe she didn't have sex with Joseph. It could be Becky didn't have schizophrenia and you don't have to worry. It could be she had a mood disorder and her pregnancy—that wash of hormones made her an exaggerated version of herself. With therapy and medications, she could have gotten better.

"It could be Becky and you have the same dad and Becky had schizophrenia and you have a higher risk of having the same health issues. Or it could be you had different fathers and are working with different heredity."

"Shit, we don't have any answers just more questions." I lowered my head to the table.

"That's quite often what happens. In the course of things, you learn there are answers you can live with better than you thought; and there are some uncertainties you can live with better than you thought. Does it really matter what Becky's precise diagnosis was?"

I stared at Mickey. I liked her muffins, but her logic baffled me at times. "Of course, it matters."

"Why? What will you do differently if you knew that Becky had schizophrenia?"

"I'd, I'd...I don't know. I have to think about it. It just makes sense to me that knowing helps me know what to expect and how to handle it. Animals are easier."

"Are animals so different? What's your process?"

It felt like an oral exam at school. I closed my eyes, took a breath, quieted my mind, and thought about the things I knew. "I look at the symptoms. I review what kinds of illnesses a particular animal is prone to get and compare the symptoms. I identify what caused the illness and choose an effective medication. I adjust the medication for the size of the animal and try it over time. I watch to see what happens and adjust based on the progress of the animal."

"Lorraine, are you ever uncertain about what is causing the illness or what's wrong?"

"Yeah, of course. Some things can be determined with laboratory tests but often I just do the best I can with the information I have and keep watch." As soon as I said it, I felt rotten. I was saying the same thing she said about the mental health professionals who treated Becky.

"It's the same for psychiatry, too, only we have fewer blood tests to confirm causes of a disease and symptoms have to be explained in words without the benefit of any visible wound or change of temperature. From the information I have, I don't think we know for certain Becky had schizophrenia. She may have had a mood disorder that included the perception that God required a sacrifice from her. Some aspects of her personality were in hyperdrive. Once the hormones of pregnancy and after pregnancy evened out, maybe Becky would have too. We needed more time to watch and adjust. We didn't get it because Becky went off her medications, got sicker, and killed herself." Mickey lightly and very briefly touched my forearm before she began talking again.

"Based on what you have told me, I would not suspect you have schizophrenia. I think you're hearing your own thoughts albeit expressed with Becky's sarcasm. She is the natural person for you to process your life with. She was your sister, your twin. She knows all the players. It fits that she is the one who expresses your self-doubts about whether you did enough to save her. Like it or not, she was a measuring stick for you. You judged your looks and performance in school, dating, friendships, relationship with your parents and God compared to what you saw in Becky. You know what Becky has said, might say, would say, should say, and could say."

I didn't say anything. Mickey was on a roll doing what I guessed she was trained to do with people. I'd hear her out. So far, she didn't seem too out in left field despite what Becky said in my head.

"You aren't the type of person to ask for assurances from the outside. You did what you needed to, and it was enough," Mickey said. "Your family is not a gushing family, falling all over you in order to make sure you are aren't wounded from what you saw, experienced, and feared. It was a dialog with Becky that makes the most sense. I think she will stop accusing you when you finally accept that you did enough. You didn't fail her."

"That's it? I need to accept that I did enough?"

"I'm not saying it's easy. You've proven you like to control things just as much as your momma."

Ouch.

She handed me a slightly bigger baby food jar. She poured the jelly beans from the little baby food jar into the larger jar and gave me the rest of the box of jelly beans. "I hope you will come here at least one more time before you leave again for school but in case you don't, take your beans with you."

I hugged Mickey quick. I didn't want to break any therapy rules. I took my jar of beans, held them up, and nodded at her. Just as I was about to get in my truck, I called back to her, "Take Tumor to see Twitch. It might be nothing, but Tumor has some abdominal growths. It doesn't have to be cancer, but you should have them checked out. I'm sorry to have to tell you that."

"Thank you, Lorraine." Mickey looked down at the smelly mutt.

"I'll be praying I'm wrong, but if Tumor does have something that can't be treated, you can count on me to help you when it's time." *When it's time.* I couldn't say the actual words.

Mickey nodded, went back into her cabin, and I left.

Chapter Seventeen

My Women

I hadn't called Marin the day before as I said I would but hadn't made it to her place or invited her to the farm. I hadn't talked with Charity again since she'd dropped me off at the hospital parking lot my first day back. Neither of them knew I had met with Lewis and had a plan to sting McGerber at sundown that night. I sat in my truck a moment looking out at Swan Lake and wondering what I'd do next.

Marin picked up on the first ring. She was working, of course. I didn't ask what tragic situation or situations in our County had her attention. Like usual she made time to talk with me.

"How's your dad? I worried when I didn't hear from you."

"He had a turn. He may have pneumonia. I slept in his room last night. He seemed better this morning and thinks he could get out on Saturday. Momma and Twitch are with him now. Frankie stayed with Ricky at his big household last night. Oh, and Frankie met somebody, Justin. I just finished my second therapy session with Mickey."

"Oh, you've had two therapy sessions already?"

It was interesting to me she found it more unbelievable I had two therapy sessions than Frankie finding a love interest in Bend. "You know us Tylers don't like to do things by half measures. When it comes to our mental health, we need daily therapy sessions. I joke, but actually, it's been good, interesting. I have a whole jar of jelly beans, the good brand."

"Jelly beans? I don't know what that means."

"It's okay. I can explain it when I see you. When will I see you?"

"I am going to be tied up most of the day and into evening. I may see you after dinner if you're free."

"I have one engagement tonight. It will keep me out after dark." I told her about my meeting with Lewis and my impending meeting with Lewis and Warren McGerber. Big mistake.

"Lorraine Tyler, meeting Lewis out in a field after dark is the most reckless, fool-headed thing you could do. What were you thinking?"

I didn't like those particular descriptors for me. "Well, I know you have lots of clients to manage today. I'll call you later." I hung up my phone and turned it off. I expected maybe Becky would chime in about then to accentuate my failings, but she was quiet. I drove to Charity's house.

I did not park down the road and sneak into the yard. I parked my truck between Pastor Grind's tan Toyota and Charity's red truck. Then, I walked up to the front door and knocked like a normal, acceptable friend and neighbor should do. Charity answered. I could see her mom and dad behind her. Pastor Grind said, "Invite Lorraine in."

Normally if I thought I heard those words I would have my hearing checked or my head further examined but the invitation was real. I walked right into the Grind house like I did all those years before when Jolene Grind was my classmate and best friend. The house smelled like apple pie. I was reminded that Mrs. Grind almost always had something baking in the oven or cooling on wooden dowel racks on the counter. Mrs. Grind was a compulsive baker. It was amazing the whole family wasn't fat and diabetic if they ate all she baked. My guess is they didn't. I suppose most of what she baked was delivered to church functions and pie-starved shut-ins.

"Lorraine, how is your dad?" Pastor Grind ushered me into the sitting room. It was one of those rooms for people who have lots of guests—a formal living room with none of the wear and tear that most of us had in our living rooms. It was tidy and dusted, no wrappers or stained couch cushions. No television. Recent issues of *National Geographic* were fanned out on the coffee table. Matching lamps flanked each end of the divan, identical armchairs in the same fabric as the couch sat invitingly but spaced at a good conversational distance. I sat in one of them knowing there was only room for me in the chair and I wouldn't be within arm's reach of Charity.

"Dad's hanging in there. Your prayers are appreciated. He had a turn yesterday. He's fighting pneumonia but was in good spirits this morning when I saw him."

"That's good news, Lorraine," Pastor Grind said. "I've gotten to know Joseph a little better over the past several weeks as we have both worked to get one more town hall meeting set up for the senate race."

Mrs. Grind offered me some pie.

I declined.

"Speaking of the senate race, Pastor Grind, there's something you should know. All of you should know it. When I ran into Warren McGerber at the gas station yesterday, he admitted to me that he beat and sexually assaulted Ricky."

Mrs. Grind gasped. Charity looked at her dad who shook his head in disbelief and horror I suppose.

"He's not going to admit it to you or the sheriff," I said. "He's convinced he's going to get away with it and become a senator representing us. I can't stand the thought of that happening."

"What are you suggesting, Lorraine?" Pastor Grind asked.

"Did Charity happen to mention my idea about you giving your support to Mrs. Jackson, the candidate running against Warren McGerber? I think it is admirable you have considered entering the race yourself. I'd hate to see you leave the church. The church needs you." Wow, I had voluntarily sought the counsel of my momma, seen a therapist, and now told Pastor Grind he was needed in the church at Bend. Maybe I wasn't crazy, I was possessed.

"Charity did tell me your idea. Intriguing. I am just not certain what to do." Pastor Grind sat on the couch and took Mrs. Grind's hand in his as he talked. "I don't want him passing off his hate as the word of God, but who am I to judge him. I've come to realize I have sounded and believed just as hateful myself until recent months."

"I don't think anyone's asking you to be judge, just another citizen. It isn't up to any one person to stop him." *Except Lewis and I are going to catch him.*

I could see he was mulling the idea over. I pushed forward. "At least come hear what Mrs. Jackson has to say at the town hall meeting tomorrow. I think it would really boost her support in Bend if you gave her your vote."

"Lorraine mentioned that another way Warren McGerber could be knocked out of the race is if those farmhands return and testify about what they know," Charity said.

"I wish we knew where to find them," Grind said.

"They're back," I said.

"What? Did they come after you, Lorraine?" Charity asked.

"No, I talked with Lewis on the phone."

Charity looked relieved.

"Then, I met with him at the Lake Tavern."

Pastor Grind put his hand to his face like he stifled a swear. "Do you think that's safe? Did you call the sheriff?"

"Lewis apologized." I waited a beat for my words to sink in, not expecting them to be received so slowly. "I didn't call the sheriff. The sheriff would have arrested him, and I need him to get Warren McGerber to confess his part in what happened to Ricky. Ricky still doesn't remember so he can't witness for himself."

Grind shook his head back and forth. "Oh, Lorraine, I doubt anyone is going to get Warren McGerber to confess."

"Well, I'll know tonight." I never stopped to think it might not be the smartest thing in the world to be disclosing my plan to trick McGerber to Pastor Grind. "At sunset tonight Lewis is meeting Warren McGerber at the approach where he beat Ricky. Lewis is going to ask for his money or threaten to tell the sheriff McGerber paid him and Petey to hold Ricky and me hostage and cut off Ricky's jaw wires early so McGerber could know if Ricky knew who beat him. Lewis is going to meet McGerber and I'm going to be there, too, hidden in the field, to record the whole thing. Then, I'll call the sheriff."

Charity and her parents looked at me with concern, possibly concern I'd lost my mind.

"What you're suggesting isn't safe." Charity came to the side of my chair and knelt there. She took my hand in front of God and her parents. "I don't think you should do this alone." She turned back to her parents, "Mom? Dad?"

"Charity is right, Lorraine. This seems like a dangerous plan."

Tell me I have God on my side. Tell me I have you on my side.

"Are you certain you can trust Lewis?" Grind asked.

I didn't mention my handy ice scraper. "I don't know for sure. All I can do is take him at his word," I said.

Grind said nothing.

"He looked genuinely sorry," I said.

Oh shit. What was I thinking? Surely someone with more sense will stop me.

Still nothing from the pastor or first lady.

I'd have to think of something for my protection, but there was no way I was telling Grind that I was afraid or backing down. I did what a lot of people did when faced with concern but no offer of help. I talked about having faith.

"I think it was you or maybe you were quoting Jesus or somebody, but you said there has to be a way back for people when they sin. There has to be the grace of forgiveness or everyone is lost." I searched their faces. The concern/are you nuts expressions dissipated to polite smiles.

Charity kept hold of my hand and lowered her cheek against my leg. I thought of how that scene would appear to anyone outside. It would look like a family having a very tender, private conversation. And it was.

I stayed for lunch. Pastor and Mrs. Grind made it clear they were worried for me but would respect my wishes to attempt this solution and of course, they'd pray. Charity and I went up to her studio apartment and I parked myself on her couch again. Charity started watching me and then sketching me.

"What time is it?" I asked as I crawled across the floor to where she sat and sketched.

"It's almost seven."

"Wow, who's that wild-haired woman?"

"Oh, just somebody I know." Charity brushed her hand against my cheek.

I remembered what she'd said about her and Kelly having gotten into patterns of running after shiny things. "Was I just a shiny thing that distracted you from your relationship with Kelly?"

"No, you weren't, aren't a shiny thing. You are my heart." She squeezed my hand and stood up quickly. I thought she would say more. "I still have one of your sweatshirts here. You should wear it if you're set on hiding in some field at night."

I took the sweatshirt and left wishing I could have stayed.

On my way to Hollister's field, I made two calls. First, I called Russ.

When Russ picked up, I said, "Don't tell Ricky I'm calling."

"Okay, I think," he said suspiciously into the phone.

"Remember when you ran away and left Ricky with those college guys and McGerber?"

"Of course, I remember, Lorraine," Russ sounded angry. "You know very well I can't forget what I did. How could you ask me that?"

"Help make up for it," I said.

"How? How can I make up for running away like a coward and Ricky getting beaten?" I could hear tears in his voice.

"Meet me in Hollister's field. Bring a flashlight and a baseball bat. Help watch my back while Lewis and I sting McGerber. I don't want Petey or some other cretin sneaking up on me."

"I'll make something up. I'll be there."

Russ disconnected the call.

Next, I called Momma's cell. I knew she'd have it off because of hospital rules but I wanted to hear her voice. I was doing just the sort of operation she would have designed if she hadn't been so busy with worrying about Dad. I listened to her message and even the Old Testament Bible verse. It was one of my favorites from the book of Jeremiah. The Israelites were complaining about all the things they were going through, and God tells them, "If it has wearied you to race with men on foot, how shall you compete with horses?" The point was to stop whining because tougher times will come, and we need to be ready for bigger challenges. In order to follow the way of God, the way of love, we have to be ready to compete with horses.

Chapter Eighteen

The Sting

Kenny's family farm had been abandoned pretty much since Becky died. The lawn was overgrown and the fences were sagging with rotting boards. The outbuildings needed paint and someone to evict the wildlife critters who were now squatting where the farm animals, feed, tools, and machinery had been. Disuse or not, the place still smelled of pig shit.

Mrs. Hollister lived in the apartments in town. She got by on her social security. She hadn't sold the farm. I believed she hoped Kenny would change his mind and be the pig farmer his tyrant father had wanted him to be. I doubted he would. The Hollister farm held ghosts for Kenny. It was there he, his mom, and siblings were bullied and battered by old man Hollister.

I thought for a moment about Kenny's dad. How many jelly beans would be in his jar for what he'd done and for what had likely been done to him to make him the kind of man who expressed anger, hate, and fear so readily with harsh words and his meaty fists. I would bet his jar was big and full.

I thought about Kenny. Like all of us he made his mistakes, but he had grown into a good dad and husband. It seemed to me he made a choice to use his words and move his hands with gentleness. It was on this land Kenny lived with the love of his life, my sister Becky. For a brief time, they had marital bliss and a new son. It must have felt like only a minute of time compared to the months following when Becky got sick and ran away. When Becky was found again it took weeks in the hospital for her to return to only a shadow of her former self. Even that pale version of Becky didn't last long before she stopped her meds and followed the messages from the imposter God in her head.

"I wanted a garden right over there," Becky said like the trip down memory lane wasn't unpleasant for her. "Little Man could have had a tire swing hung from the largest oak tree. It's okay though. He's got a nice wooden swing set where he's living with his dad...and momma, Ramona."

I parked in the Hollister yard, cut the engine and lights. Kenny's dad's ghost probably walked that farm along with the ghosts of slaughtered pigs. I only needed to make my way across the yard and through a small grove of trees to the bigger field, where two hundred yards in I would hide and wait for Lewis's call when Warren McGerber arrived at the gated approach. I planned to join Lewis after the sting and have him drive me back to my truck. I didn't want to linger at the Hollister farm. It was creepy.

I pictured Lewis and me driving together to the sheriff's office. Maybe we'd take his truck since his passenger door actually opened. Dispatch could alert Sheriff Scrogrum that we were there to provide evidence in the open hate crime case involving Ricky Johnson.

In my mind I pictured the sheriff after having heard the recording of Warren McGerber's confession assembling a posse of sorts to find and capture McGerber. Each person in the posse thanked Lewis and me and told us how brave and honorable we had been. It would have been cool to ride horses. Perhaps, I'd be deputized. Film at eleven.

I was right about the film at eleven, but there were no horses. A horse's ass, yes, but no horses.

It seemed like an endless stream of cars and trucks approached but didn't stop at the gated approach where Lewis had parked his gray truck. I knelt in the weeds, watched, and waited for starlit evening. Grasshoppers landed on me with their Velcro legs. I imagined them spitting their brown chaw on my clothes. The heat of the day had gone home, the air was cooling, and bats flew overhead, slicing the sky as they devoured mosquitoes and the other churring insects of the night. I changed positions often and was immediately colder than I'd expected, more from excitement and fear than the actual temperature.

"This isn't going to work," Becky said.

Lewis had turned off his headlights but had a flashlight he tried by pointing the lamp at his face and flipping the switch. He looked ghoulish in that light and this vision added to my mounting fear and dread as he grinned and looked out into the field where we agreed I'd be.

My phone rang. Lewis's voice came through the speaker loud and clear. "It's almost showtime. There's a black truck slowing down. I think it's him. Can you hear me?"

"Yeah, I hear you. I'm in position. Good luck."

It's cliché but time slowed down. I rubbernecked, looking behind me, praying for Russ's backup and worrying that Petey would arrive instead and kill me with the bolt cutters we'd used to dehorn McGerber's bull.

It took forever for Warren to park his truck in the approach next to Lewis's truck.

I listened on the open phone line from my position.

"My, don't you look senatorial in your fancy suit," Lewis addressed Warren McGerber.

I could picture what Lewis was describing, possibly mocking. I'd seen it for myself earlier in the week. In public Warren McGerber wore western styled suits with finely tooled leather boots and pressed shirts with mother-of-pearl buttons or snaps. He gave the impression of power, business, and earned authority. It was his costume.

"Lewis, it's nice to see you again," Warren said.

"Is it?"

I looked over my shoulder toward the Hollister farm. Still no sign of Russ.

When I looked back to Lewis, Warren had moved closer. "It's been a long time. I trust you are well."

I felt confused. McGerber behaved like he was attending a class reunion. Had Warren's classmates predicted he was the man most likely to nearly beat a man to death?

Then, I heard rustling in the weeds behind me. Oh, shit.

"Russ?"

No answer. More crunching weeds.

What was that? A bear? Worse yet maybe Warren McGerber had fooled us both and Petey or one of McGerber's newly enlisted henchmen was sneaking up to kill me. Throw another bean in the jar. I didn't know whether to scream, run, fight, or just close my eyes as the creature got closer. *Shit, shit, shit.* I didn't want to mess up our sting operation.

I could hear McGerber asking after Petey like he and Lewis were old friends. Maybe they were.

Of course, they're friends. They're peas in a pod. Why did I expect anything else?

My throat was dry and when I was just about to pass out from fear, what sky I could see was blocked by a body, and then the body was on top of mine and a hand covered my mouth.

I flailed my arms and inhaled air through my nose. Just as I was about to punch and kick, I smelled strawberries.

"Shhh, Raine, it's me, Charity."

I'd nearly wet myself.

"Holy Christ, what are you doing here?" Luckily, the volume was muted on my side of the open line or Lewis and Warren McGerber would have gotten an earful and I would have lost my position.

"I was worried about you."

Isn't that about the sweetest thing in the world? I would have appreciated it more if my heart wasn't beating like I'd been dosed with speed. I couldn't catch my breath.

I shushed her. "I'm listening to Warren McGerber." Her body was still on top of mine, her face only inches away. I swallowed hard. I forgot for a moment what I was doing there. "We need to record his confession."

"Let's get at it then." She rolled off me and we both listened to Lewis and McGerber.

She barely got the words out when Russ arrived. He carried two aluminum baseball bats for which I was grateful. Ricky, Frankie, and Justin stumbled along behind Russ, for which I was perturbed. Right behind them, Grind and Marin arrived. My God, it was a circus. Marin wedged herself between Charity and me. Pastor Grind got on the ground by Charity. Ricky, Russ, and Frankie wrestled for positions to see the action.

There was whispering and shushing that made more noise than the words being shushed. I learned they all had been worried about me, my safety. Ricky said, "You don't have to do everything on your own, Lorraine." He looked over at Russ and put his head on his shoulder. "This guy can't keep a secret from me ever. Frankie has been telling us about ways to use friends and allies. You should try it for a change, Lorraine."

I felt really good inside thinking about having a posse of people who worried about me enough to hide in a field in the dark with me. So, of course I said, "Would all of you just shut up. I'm trying to record a confession here."

"I want my money," Lewis said.

The fact Lewis and McGerber were still talking and not paying attention to the convention in the field seemed like a miracle to me.

"I can see how you need money, Lewis." Warren controlled the conversation more than I liked. "From what you've told me during our wonderful conversations at the Lake Tavern you have aspirations to have your own farm. Is that right?"

Lewis stepped closer to Warren. "I want the money you owe me."

"Of course, you have some loose ends to tie up before you can begin any kind of new life. I suppose you want a chance to apologize to Ricky and of course, Lorraine. Have you done that yet, Lewis?"

Lewis mumbled something I didn't catch.

Becky said, "This is bad. It's not going to work."

"Maybe, you've talked with them already. Good for you, Lewis. Amends is a good first step."

I wanted to put my first step right up Warren McGerber's ass.

"What are you talking about, McGerber? Did you apologize..." Lewis tried to guide the conversation, but he was outmatched. Flustered I suppose, he blurted, "Have you stopped cheating on your wife?"

McGerber cut Lewis off. "I think the important thing is everyone needs a new start. I know you feel badly about hurting Ricky and Lorraine."

Lewis didn't speak right away but eventually fell into the call and response that McGerber had constructed. "Yes, I want them to know I'm sorry for what I did."

"Good, Lewis. Admitting our wrongs is a good start. You admit that you hurt Ricky and Lorraine. I think that's what you're saying?"

Weakly, Lewis said, "Yes."

Damn it. What was happening? This wasn't how it was supposed to go. I looked around at my allies. They were as confused and worried as I was. I struggled to my knees. "No, no, no."

"Told you," Becky said.

I wanted to run to Lewis from where I hid and tell him to shut up. Quit confessing. Before I could stand sirens ruptured the relative quiet and the flashing lights of the sheriff's cruiser lit the night sky. It was a trap. Lewis and I hadn't stung McGerber; McGerber had stung Lewis.

*

I ran toward Lewis. I didn't look back to see how many of my posse were following. Even through the night lit by emergency vehicle lights and headlights I could see the panic in Lewis's face as he moved toward his truck. The sheriff's car blocked Lewis's truck from the back and the gate blocked him from driving the truck forward. He saw me when I was almost to the fence line.

Lewis screamed at me, "Why? Lorraine? We had a deal." Sheriff Scrogrum put cuffs on him.

"No," I rasped.

Warren McGerber rushed over to me as I climbed over the gate. The sheriff read Lewis his rights. McGerber put his arm around my shoulder and pulled me close, his nails biting into my upper arm, a grin pasted on his smug face. "You did the right thing, Lorraine. It's time for Lewis to take responsibility."

"You bastard! Lewis is here to tell what you did." I pulled away from him. He just smiled. He didn't seem worried about anyone believing what I said.

More headlights—a TV van screeched to a stop, the doors slid open, and a camera crew and reporters piled out to film the sheriff restraining and arresting Lewis. Someone, maybe from McGerber's campaign, had a small platform, lights on stands, and microphones. McGerber took the stage as Lewis continued yelling profanity and accusations of betrayal at me. I tried to work my way to the sheriff.

When I was finally close enough where I thought the sheriff could hear me, I shouted, "Sheriff, Sheriff, you've got it mixed up. It's Lewis who has information about who beat Ricky."

"I bet he does. I'll hear all about it when I take him in on this warrant. We got his compadre, Petey, already in the pokey. We caught him trying to meet up with his girl."

The sheriff helped Lewis duck his head as he stuffed him in the backseat of the cruiser. His cowboy hat had fallen to the ground. I picked it up. I stood by the car pounding my hands on the side window and yelling to Lewis, "I didn't call the sheriff. McGerber did this." Lewis turned his face away from me. McGerber had stung us both.

As the cameras turned to where Warren McGerber perched on a wooden stage in his cowboy suit, he took cards from his coat pocket. He had a planned speech. This was a staged photo opportunity for him. I rushed toward him to disrupt his broadcast but as if my every move was anticipated, two large men I didn't recognize stopped my forward progress and then whisked me into the air like I weighed nothing and spirited me back across the gravel and over the fence into the field back from where I'd come. "Get!" the larger man spit at me.

Where was I supposed to go?

Charity was there. Marin was there. Ricky was crying and Russ held him. Frankie stood on the other side of the fence with shock frozen on her face. She came over to me and whispered, "Ricky's really shook up. I think he's getting flashbacks of the beating."

I didn't wish Ricky the pain of remembering but I selfishly wanted some way to get McGerber to feel pain and terror.

Pastor Grind was missing. I wondered where he went. When Charity stepped forward and wiped my face with her shirt sleeve, I realized I'd been crying.

Marin said, "I've been calling and texting you. Why didn't you answer?"

I turned to Marin. "Is Dad okay?"

"He's fine as far I know. I was trying to warn you that Petey got arrested. Addie heard the sheriff say he planned to scoop up Lewis tonight."

Shit.

Ricky remembers.

Charity said, "While you ran off to stop the sheriff, Dad lit out in the other direction."

"Yeah, what did he say?" I asked as she took my hand.

"He said he needed to call some people and that we shouldn't to give up hope."

"Sounds like something a good dad would say. Speaking of which. I want to go see mine."

Chapter Nineteen

Our Father

When I got to Dad's room he was still on oxygen. Twitch sat on one side of his bed in the recliner I'd slept in the night before. Momma wasn't in the room.

"I just told your dad about your adventure out in Hollister's field," Twitch said.

"How did you hear about that?" I don't know why it surprised me Twitch knew about me being out in the Hollister field. Didn't news always travel fast and even faster when it was bad news. My escapade in Hollister's field made it back to Langston Hospital faster than I could drive my truck there.

"I think the whole town has heard. McGerber credits you with bringing two dangerous felons to justice. Of course, McGerber being McGerber he took most of the credit for himself. He's a real law and order candidate, cowboy suit and all."

"Yeah, well, don't believe everything you hear," I said, but I felt more shame at my misadventure than I felt hope.

"What really happened, Lorraine?" Dad and Twitch both looked at me.

"I'm sorry to say that your one remaining daughter was outfoxed. Lewis and I had planned to record McGerber confessing to beating Ricky. Instead, McGerber had the sheriff waiting in the weeds to arrest Lewis. In truth, it was me waiting in the weeds. The sheriff was in a bug-free car sitting on upholstered seats waiting to pounce on Lewis once Lewis admitted he hurt Ricky and me."

"Lewis was arrested? I suppose that's some good news. He and Petey were awfully rough on you and Ricky," Dad said around the oxygen mask before he put it back on his face.

"Dad doesn't need to be bothered with this, Lorraine. He's sick," Becky said.

"It's Warren McGerber who needs to be arrested," I said. "Well, truth be told they should both be arrested. There's room for Petey in a cell with them. Now Lewis thinks I sold him out and Warren looks like a brave candidate for congress. It just slays me. I helped his campaign." I slapped my hand against my jeans and felt the box of jelly beans. I took out the box and handed a jelly bean each to Dad and Twitch.

"I don't know if what happened counts as a trauma against me, but I can tell you that it feels awful."

"These are the good brand," Dad said.

Then they just looked at me like I was crazy but didn't say it. They both ate their bean.

Chapter Twenty

The Town Hall

Bend held this newly scheduled, last town hall in the late afternoon so other evening civic events like softball leagues, fishing, drinking at the town pub or watching TV and movies were not disrupted. Boys and girls high school sports had ended for the year. The Minnesota Wild hockey team was off. Vikings weren't playing or at training camp. Several of them were facing court dates for sexual assault, speeding, and gun possession. The Timberwolves hadn't made the play-offs even though in professional basketball half the teams did. The Twins were experiencing poor pitching. Most folks still didn't believe that Minnesota had a professional women's basketball team. Maybe these professional sports foibles made it easier for Dad and his supporters to get another town hall scheduled.

No more names could be added to the ballot for the senate seat in our district after the end of June. The rest of the campaign would run its course through the remaining days of summer into fall without debates or big events. It was get in now or stay out of the way. Grind still hadn't put his hat in the ring so for now, Warren McGerber—recently recognized local hero—was fighting against Allison Jackson—a Black woman who might also be Muslim—for the senate spot representing our district.

As Bend goes, so votes the district was a bit of an exaggeration. The same could be said for most of the small towns in the district except for Browerville and Upsala who often got it wrong. The district, like most of rural Minnesota, voted as a Republican block and generally voted for the least offensive Republican on the ballot or the candidate they thought would most likely win. To have voted for a Democrat was perceived as a vote for higher taxes and no one admitted they favored that even though they complained about the "goddamned roads" and lack of affordable health insurance.

The actual meeting itself would take place at Bend High School auditorium which was big enough—not that many people go; it's accessible—theatre seating on one level; it was an important civic event—there would be free snacks and beverages. This town hall was significant because it was an extra meeting solicited by voters and now, there was a promise of TV cameras from a small area station and possibly from some network affiliates in the Twin Cities because a local man was making a big splash in his quest to bring God to the Minnesota State Senate. The attraction was compounded by the news coverage from the evening before when Warren McGerber had risked his life to bring a fugitive to justice.

I didn't know if this media attention was as much an endorsement of his beliefs and politics as an attempt for viewership by putting something cute, odd, or gross on TV. For me he wasn't like the cute raccoon who climbed the Metro skyscraper. McGerber was a rabid skunk who was ready to misrepresent good people and infect and stink up an entire state government.

Warren showed up early. I watched from a spot in the shadows of the balcony. I'd sat up there as a member of the pep band for boys' basketball games. I credit the embouchure I attained playing the coronet for my exceptional kissing ability. The stage and court looked so small. At the same time, the stage had hosted basketball and volleyball games, school plays, Memorial Day remembrances, concerts from beginning bands and choirs to final senior performances that capped off a year of pride and loyalty to the school and Bend, the town itself. It was fitting that this campaign would come to a head on this stage.

My warm reminiscence was interrupted and obliterated when Becky piped up, "I was a cheerleader on that very court."

"Shut up. I'm depressed already," I said out loud not worrying who might hear me.

When McGerber pranced up the steps to the stage and stood preening behind the podium I wished I had a rifle. That's not true. I didn't wish for a rifle, but I did want a way to stop him and at that moment I was feeling pretty impotent to do so. Maybe it was this type of hopelessness that allowed some people to skip the moral inventory they'd have to ignore to become the unidentified shooters in the ever-growing phenomenon of mass shootings. Ironically, most of those shooters were white males and it was mostly white males in leadership. Why did they feel so impotent?

Charity planned to talk with her dad again and suggest to him this would be the prime and last public opportunity for him to announce he was running himself or put his support behind Allison Jackson. He needed to decide.

The smell of real buttered popcorn wafted into the air. Nothing like salt and hot oil to bring a crowd. The seats began filling. I saw paper bags of popcorn, paper cups of pop, and dessert bars on paper napkins filling the hands of would-be voters. The chatter between neighbors steadily increased in numbers and volume. I saw Allison Jackson arrive. She had a group of supporters with her which was wise. I hustled down the balcony steps holding the railing so that I could get down to her before she was too near McGerber. She dropped a poster, and I was able to help pick it up and get her attention.

"Hi, Mrs. Jackson, you don't know me, but I am voting for you and I just wanted to say it's really important you don't let him win." I nodded toward Warren McGerber. I suppose there were dumber things I could have said.

"I do plan to win. What's your name?" She put out her hand to me.

I took her hand and shook it and smiled like an idiot seeing the fair for the first time. "I'm Lorraine Tyler. I just need you to know if Warren McGerber gets into government, he will build his public policy based on hate and fear. He doesn't represent who we are."

She took my arm. "Are you able to stay for the meeting? Would you sit up front near me?" she asked.

My face flushed. "It might not help you, being associated with me. I'm queer."

Just then a ruckus broke out behind us as Frankie, Russ, Ricky, and Justin, with Allan on his shoulders, entered with their posters. On their heels a group of twenty or more people pushed through the auditorium doors holding PFLAG signs and rainbow flags. There were smiles and laughing and staring and whispers all mixed together as people entered the Bend auditorium. I waved at friends and neighbors.

Russ caught my eye and mouthed that he needed to talk to me.

I yelled that I'd see them after the meeting. I still had some things to tell Allison Jackson.

"I'm hoping Pastor Grind is going to get here and say something so people know McGerber doesn't speak for all the hearts of this town, but I see there's some other people who will help make sure every voice is heard." I wiped tears from my eyes watching the mix of people milling about and moving toward the snacks and empty seats.

Allison Jackson's smile was so beautiful, and she listened to me. She let go of my arm and said, "I invite you to sit up front with my family and I would be most grateful to meet your friends."

What a simple, incredible, had-to-hear-it-to-compare-it-to-the-dumbass thing to say. This was why it was important to have good people run for public office. She made me feel a part of things and welcome. Neither democracy nor civility had died. It may have panicked and paused but it had not died. I sat in one of the front seats next to kids who I assumed were her children. A boy, maybe twelve looked at me, "Are you here to see my mom?"

"Yes, I am. She told me I could sit here."

"She shake your hand yet?" he asked.

"Yes, she did. She's beautiful."

"I think she is too." He pointed to where his mom was shaking hands with Warren McGerber. "See that?"

"You mean McGerber?"

"Yeah, that's his name. He looks like he's taking my mom's power when he holds her hand but he's wrong. My mom has got him. He has no power over her." The young man smiled and adored his momma from where he sat.

I don't know that I understood exactly what he meant but I believed him. The event was ready to start. Charity and her dad took the last remaining seats in the front before TV cameras and microphones, lighting techs, and campaign staff filled the space between where we were sitting and the stage. I scanned the auditorium for Marin and Twitch. I wished Dad could have been there since he made it happen. I would go to the hospital directly after the town hall and tell him all about it.

Mrs. Swisher, the former civics instructor, introduced the candidates and explained the format for the meeting. Everyone should get their snacks and drinks and sit. The boys and girls scout troops would present the colors—both the US flag and the flag of Minnesota. We would join together for the Pledge of Allegiance. Each candidate would make a brief statement and then the floor would be open for questions from the assembly. Microphones had been strategically placed on the aisles for people to make their question heard. Each candidate would have no more than two minutes to respond. There was to be no foul language, name calling, interrupting or talking over other speakers.

I admired the thoughtfulness and sense of fair play that went into the planning but had very little hope this meeting wouldn't soon devolve into mean-spirited mud wrestling. I was so glad there was popcorn.

McGerber took the stage for his opening comments right after the pledge. He stood with hands on his hips as the scouts were shuffling to the edge of the stage. Suddenly, one boy with a flagpole in one hand stopped and pointed at McGerber. Like dominoes the scouts ran into one another almost falling, but not before the boy yelled, "Gun." The rest of the flag-bearing, allegiance-blurting children dropped to the floor and scuttled for hiding spots like they had been drilled to do because of the contagion of school shootings.

I looked more closely at what the scout had scouted. Sure enough, McGerber, the idiot, was wearing a gun in his waistband.

The boy who had pointed was still upright, frozen in position, and had wet himself. A dark stain crawled along his freshly pressed brown best pants down his legs to his recently polished white gym shoes. One of the boys, not so bright, tried to hide behind McGerber's legs missing the point that he had brought himself closer to the potential shooter.

In the panic McGerber, the dumbass, raised the gun into the air trying to make light of it and shouted into his now screeching microphone, "I'm a law-and-order candidate and not afraid to fight for what is right." His stance echoed his lawn posters that boasted of "boots on the ground to protect the American family."

Who would protect families from McGerber with a firearm?

Then I saw it. Warren McGerber had his hand in the air waving a handgun. He raised his left arm to motion for the crowd to be quiet. His sleeve pulled back from his wrist. His left wrist had a crescent shaped tattoo or birthmark just like Ricky had dreamed about.

Sheriff Scrogrum had moved closer to the dais. His hands were on his utility belt and his jaw was slack as he moved forward.

"Sheriff," I said in one of those half-assed whisper shouts. I moved to him hoping he wouldn't misunderstand the situation and shoot me. "Ricky remembered that the man who beat him had a half-moon birthmark on his left wrist. Warren McGerber has one. I saw it."

The Sheriff glared at me and then at McGerber. The cogs in the sheriff's brain turned ever so slowly, propelled by small squirrels I presumed. Suddenly, he bolted up the center aisle of the school auditorium as if he'd been shot out of a canon. Despite his unprecedented demonstration of speed Allison Jackson had already removed the gun from Warren McGerber's outstretched hand and unloaded the weapon, bullets splashing in the flag bearer's pooled urine. McGerber was frozen in place.

Many people in the crowd were standing—some leaving and others pressing closer to the stage. I felt a tug on my arm and looked up to find Russ standing over me.

"Ricky got more of his memory back. He told me about the dream he keeps having of the man who beat him. Ricky remembered. Not that we're ever going to get Warren McGerber to show his wrist."

He already did. I got him.

I rushed onto the stage and approached the Sheriff again. Sheriff Scrogrum had McGerber's gun tucked in his own belt by this time.

"Sheriff, check his wrist," I said. "Ricky remembers. The man who beat him has a birthmark shaped like a crescent moon."

The sheriff was already holding McGerber by the arm. He pulled up McGerber's sleeve on his left hand. He then nodded to two deputies who mounted the stage and grabbed McGerber.

I heard the sheriff say, "Well, Mr. Law and Order, you're under arrest for the beating of Ricky Johnson." The sheriff clicked his cuffs over the claret birthmark on McGerber's wrist.

In all likelihood, the trial might have taken longer than the election and McGerber would have maybe gotten off when judged by a jury of his own peers, but for some reason, he lost all composure. He didn't heed the advice to remain silent and wait for a lawyer. Maybe his hate was like a festering boil. He could not hold it in or channel it to a more secret location. He erupted and spewed hate in every direction. His every word filmed by the TV crew.

"You ignorant cattle, you would allow yourself to be led by this—this Black woman. Why not elect the faggots too. And whatever the hell you call that—" He pointed at Frankie. "You make me sick. You haven't heard the last of me. You've got no proof of anything." He glared at the sheriff, "You, you fat oaf, you'd take the word of dirty farmhands and queers over me?"

Sheriff Scrogrum tightened the cuffs. McGerber winced. "Get him out of here."

Mrs. Swisher whispered something to Allison Jackson and then took the microphone.

"People, people, if I could have your attention. There are still lots of bars, pop, and popcorn left. Get your refreshments and we will start again in two minutes. I want to give Sheriff Scrogrum a moment to explain what happened and then we will have a short address by Ms. Jackson and possibly another candidate will speak briefly."

She successfully used the information the sheriff would provide as a cliff-hanger to keep the audience. Murmurs rippled through the crowd even as people raised Rice Krispie treats and Nut Goodie bars to their mouths. There was no way in hell people were going to sit down again or be quiet again.

Sheriff Scrogrum took the microphone. *Tap, tap. Screech. Squeal.*

The sheriff's face reddened. He looked like the boy who wet his pants. "I can only say there has been a new development in the investigation of the hate crime against Ricky Johnson. A new witness has come forward and identified Warren McGerber as a person of interest in the beating of Ricky Johnson. At this time, we have taken Mr. McGerber into custody for further questioning."

He handed the microphone to Mrs. Swisher who handed it to Pastor Grind. I sat down.

Pastor Grind was probably the most experienced orator in the joint except for maybe Mrs. Jackson. Still, he stood awkwardly behind the microphone, not looking up right away, but bowing his head in silence. I thought he would pray and maybe he did silently, but in a few moments, it was quiet in the auditorium. Maybe a child asked a question or for more popcorn or a man cleared his throat, but it was quiet like a church.

When Pastor Grind lifted his head, he did not smile. He did not wear the face of a smug man, who claimed special standing with God. His eyes were red and teary. He pushed away the podium with the microphone.

Instead, he removed his suit coat, loosened his tie, and sat down on the edge of the stage. His feet dangled—not long enough to touch the auditorium floor from where he sat.

He said, "Every nation has its shame. I'll say it again, every nation has its shame. The United States of America must live with having systematically robbed, killed, and erased the first nations. Then as aliens on this land our ancestors captured and enslaved Africans to build a nation but not share in its rights or riches.

"It is good that we have short lives and memories because to remember all we have done or benefitted from is to be very ashamed. Such a short time ago our great grandparents and grandparents—Swedes, Norwegians, Poles, Irish, Germans, Finlanders, the English, the Dutch, Scottish men and women and more peoples than I can remember to list—were new to this country and treated poorly, distrusted for their differences and ignored in our similarities. Our ancestors didn't speak the language, they made and craved strange foods, and the first settlers weren't sure if these immigrants had a good enough work ethic. Wouldn't they just steal and suck the teat of the true Americans?" He smiled.

"How quickly we have forgotten those insults and instead hurl similar suspicions on another group of people coming to America for a better life like it was fine for us but the invitation has expired. Has the Statue of Liberty crossed her arms over her chest and closed her eyes? No."

At this point in his address I watched him rise.

"Every nation, every state, district, and town has its shame but all those actions began on an individual, personal level where one person at a time had to decide what they would do. All of us inherited and benefitted from the tyranny of a previous generation. Let *us* be a generation that learns from our mistakes, our shame." He spread his hands including everyone in the building.

"I come to you today at this moment not as a pastor, but as a man, a failed man. I have failed in judging others, even my own neighbors and daughter." He looked at Charity and over to me. "I asked to speak here today to say I pledge to do better."

He took a breath and swallowed but his voice still cracked when he spoke again. "I make a pledge beginning with my support for Allison Jackson for senator in our district. I am personally voting for Mrs. Jackson because she is smart, she understands how to write and enact policy, and she conducts herself with grace and integrity even when faced with hate and distrust. She embodies the qualities I want to see lead this town, this district, this state, and nation. My vote goes to Jackson."

I cheered. I cheered like my dad told me to cheer. He would be surprised to know I cheered for Grind, not just Jackson, but I cheered. I can't say the crowd went wild—it wasn't like it was a football or basketball game. Hell, we cry and gloat when we beat Browerville or Upsala. This was just a town hall meeting. The crowd didn't go wild except for the PFLAG group. The queers, the freaks, and their allies were loud.

Charity and I went wild cheering. I know we were both so proud of Pastor Grind and what he risked in admitting he had judged others including us unfairly. The audience munched on their snacks and clapped or cheered some when their hands and jaws were free. The excitement was over and a post sugar rush coma was coming fast. They nodded a lot which is a good sign in Bend.

I hadn't noticed but sometime during all this I had taken Charity's hand or maybe she took mine. We both cried as we hooted for her dad and Allison Jackson and maybe for ourselves.

Mrs. Jackson took the microphone. She said, "Thank you, Pastor Grind, for those heartfelt, wise words. Thank you, everyone, for coming. I also have a pledge. I pledge to earn your trust. I pledge I can be counted on to represent your truest hearts in my work in the senate. Good day."

I suspect her brevity bought her some votes. She didn't hold this audience captive and extol herself. She said she would earn our trust and represent our best selves. I don't know how the news media felt about the chaotic, short town hall meeting but I thought it was epic. Charity and I hugged. I hugged Grind and Mrs. Jackson, all her children and her husband. I hugged the boy who had wet himself.

Chapter Twenty-One

It Feels Like I'd Won Something

I scanned the auditorium for my posse. I caught Ricky and Russ's eye from across the crowd and pumped my fist in the air. They were with Frankie who was dancing next to Justin and close to where Twitch was standing. Twitch whispered something in Frankie's ear before she looked up at me. Twitch looked at me. Then Frankie said something to Justin, Ricky, and Russ. Russ took Allan from Justin's arms and held Allan to his chest. They looked at me. Twitch walked toward me making his way through the crowd. Behind him Marin had arrived and hugged Ricky and Frankie until they talked to her and she looked at me. They all walked closer. They didn't run. I wasn't on fire.

Charity was next to me. "What's wrong?" she asked, her voice sounding like it was coming from underwater.

I squeezed her hand, pulled it to my face and kissed it, but then dropped her hand. I kept my eye contact with Twitch. He nodded ever so slightly as he closed the distance between us. I couldn't look at the others because they knew, and I didn't yet, and it needed to be Twitch to say.

Ricky would have justice. McGerber, Lewis, and Petey would be charged. Allison Jackson would be the next senator of our district. None of it mattered a goddamn.

When Twitch reached me, I suppose he said something. The others were probably talking too. Knowing that crew, they were all speaking at once. I can't remember their words or voices. I just remember Twitch took me into his arms, and I lifted myself on tippy-toe. I felt hair against my face. For a moment I flashed on the Warner Sallman painting in the Sunday school room—the one of the head of Christ like he'd posed for a graduation picture. Twitch's hair and beard were softer than I remembered from the other time he'd hugged me. He smelled like soap and maybe a man's cologne—nothing strong or spicy; his breath was warm as his words vibrated against my neck.

"He's gone."

Chapter Twenty-Two

Hospital Census Down One

The landscape on the ride back to Langston hospital fluttered by the window of Twitch's truck like cartoon frames without sound or color. I was eyes only and everything was a blur.

Later I would learn I had refused to let anyone come with me and Twitch and that I had originally insisted I'd drive myself until Twitch took my keys away and tossed them to Frankie who threw them down the sewer grate outside the high school. I would hear that Ricky, Frankie, Marin, and Charity corralled me and Justin picked me up and stuffed me into Twitch's truck like a child throwing a tantrum. The gang followed Twitch and me separately in Ricky's car all the way to Langston.

I suppose they followed me to Dad's room. It seems logical. I don't remember them there. The machines were gone, I suppose. They were made unnecessary and the tether broken. I remember Momma. She was sitting in the fatigue-green Naugahyde geriatric recliner Nurse Faison had scored for Momma's comfort the first night.

Momma was sitting holding Dad in her arms on her lap as if he were her child. She rocked him and cried. Her gown and his gown were wet with tears and snot.

"Don't try to get him away from her," Twitch whispered to me. "She's not ready yet."

Twitch went into the room and stood behind Momma. He didn't touch her or Dad. He stood.

"Momma?"

She petted Dad. She cried. She petted him some more.

"Momma?"

Momma looked up. I don't know if she recognized me. "Shhh, he's sleeping now. He couldn't get his air. That part-time nurse, she didn't know what to do. Put the blessed blood pressure cuff over his IV. Nurse Faison will have her head for the mistake. Could have used that port for something to calm him." She continued rocking him.

I walked closer.

"Twitch? Where is the man?" Momma looked to the side.

"The better question is where were you, Lorraine?" Becky said.

"I'm right here, Peggy," he said from beside Momma. He put his hand on Momma's shoulder.

"Oh, I thought you'd gone. Get me a blanket. Joseph is getting so cold. He'll catch..."

Momma caught herself.

Twitch came around Momma and I came forward and without a word she let us lift Dad back into his hospital bed. Maybe Momma helped. Maybe Becky helped too. He was so weightless like all the substance of him had left with his final breath some time before. I tucked blankets around him from one side of the bed. Twitch did the same from the other side. We didn't cover his face. I kissed his cool cheek feeling stubble against my lips and leaving tears on him that I wiped away like I feared they would tickle his skin.

"At least he died in bed and not on the toilet," I said to Twitch having remembered some odd trivia that Dad had once told me. "That's something I guess." I sat in the chair next to Dad's bed. "McGerber was arrested by the sheriff for beating Ricky." I said this to him like it mattered. "Ricky got his memory back. That's a double-edged sword I suppose. Dolphins are supposed to be the animal with the best memory. You probably knew already. I thought it was elephants. I was wrong."

"Again," Becky said.

Tears streamed down my face and I don't know how long Momma and Twitch let me go on talking to Dad telling him what things happened during the day and useless animal facts I had learned in school. It was all useless in the scheme of things. It was ear wax, but I kept talking like talking held him to earth with me, like silence would swallow him whole and he'd be gone.

Sometime in there somebody made me leave. Everybody had their roles to play. I was just the daughter.

Momma was just the wife. Twitch was a friend of the family. The medical people took Dad, the patient, newly assigned role of deceased and they had him now because there were things that needed to be done to him to protect the sensibilities of the rest of the cast. We couldn't touch him anymore.

I tried to tell myself he wasn't in his body anymore, but I didn't know where to place him. Was he hovering in the room or back at the farm? Was he with Becky?

I didn't know where Dad was, but I knew exactly where to find Becky. Becky was again in my head saying how despicable it was that I had chosen a political rally over being with my father at the time of his death. Her voice was softer. Alongside her litany of my failures all the information I knew about the bodily processes of dying came into my head unbidden and unrelenting.

I couldn't treat Dad as a science project. I didn't care to know if his pupils had dilated or if his brain had continued to have firings. I had no need to see his back and buttocks where his blood pooled because he no longer had a beating heart pushing it through his body oxygenating him. His skin probably looked bruised there compared to the paleness of his face and hands. I didn't need to see it. I refused to think about the unseen bacteria in his body digesting his intestines first and later the rest of his organs. I didn't want to see him when he shits the bed.

People expect the cast of grievers to talk. I remembered this from when Becky died. People seem to crave meaningful utterances from the bereaved even if the words are slathered and drowning in tears and snot. Crying makes others and the crier uncomfortable. Death is an acceptable occasion for crying. Still, words were expected too.

I didn't have any words. I didn't want to talk. I didn't want anyone talking to me. If they talked to me, they were going to say something stupid or unnecessary. It wasn't just likely, it was probable, and I didn't think I could muster the energy to take care of them and their stupid mistakes right then.

They meant well but harm and mistakes were the only reasonable outcomes for trying to talk about something for which there were no words. I viewed their words, their sentences and paragraphs, like a battlefield and I wanted to pick off these opposing soldiers until there were only a few left standing amongst the drivel and dead of what they intended to say. Those lone survivors I could possibly hear. In truth, I'd rather they'd shut up or better yet just look into my eyes and nod because they know what it is like to lose someone and there are no words.

Chapter Twenty-Three

Aftershock

Momma, who finally went home to our farmhouse, didn't make it past the kitchen table where she sat in her chair and stared at Dad's empty spot. I hovered expecting her to cuss him out even in his absence.

"Momma? Momma?" I kept my distance even though what I wanted most in the world was to hug her. Go figure. "Momma? Can I get you anything?"

I was a highly trained observer when it came to reading nonverbal skills. Dad said it was because of all the Swedish heritage I had behind me. He said Swedes didn't say much, they held the heat of passion and disappointment inside hoping it would clear the arteries they had clogged with too much butter and white sauce.

I saw Momma shake her head ever so slightly. There was nothing she wanted right then that I had the power or authority to give her.

Again, Twitch materialized. I hadn't heard his truck in the yard or the spank of the screen door closing. The dogs lay on the kitchen floor beneath Dad's chair like they'd been drugged. Maybe they had. Maybe a certain kind of knowing left them prostrate and silent.

"I suppose there's things we've got to do. Funeral things," I said to Momma.

"Funeral things are done," Twitch said, "unless there's something you want to add to the service. I suppose some folks put up photo collages on bulletin boards or project pictures on a screen."

"How did things get done? Is there a..." I couldn't bring myself to say the word.

"You know your dad. He didn't want you throwing away good money on sentiment. He picked one out himself." Perhaps Twitch couldn't say the word either.

Twitch was right, of course. Dad had said that funeral planning should never be done by grieving people. He'd told me, "Grievers become spineless. It's a wonder they can remain upright and walk. Add to that, they feel every grief of their life like it's all happening again." Dad could have been a therapist, I think. How did he know this stuff? Maybe he, too, had a jar filled with jelly beans. He would have bought the cheaper brand.

No surprise that Dad's wisdom on grief came with an animal story. He told me how dolphins and whales have been known to tend to their dead, carry them about, and bring them to the surface for air. Primates show a continuum of grief response like people. It wasn't unusual for them to carry around a dead infant, grooming it like it was alive. Then again, primates might also pull the hair of the dead, mount the dead body, or eat it. I liked to think our species had evolved from those practices, but it was hard for me to think about funerals.

Twitch took up the slack for my cowardice. "Your dad didn't want you or your momma to feel like you needed to prove your love through the purchase of what he would have called 'ostentatious baubles.'"

Dad was no fool and he would not allow our cadre of blubbering messes to succumb to the temptation to display our affections for him through bankruptcy. He had given Twitch instructions on his funeral accommodations. Twitch showed me a picture of what Dad had chosen for *it*.

He had chosen a coffin just one step above a large appliance box and one step below the large rubber bins at Walmart in which he would have fit. The container Dad chose would not require burping, but I could swear I could read the word Maytag under the brown paint that in a certain light resembled oak paneling. The casket lacked the Dutch door and didn't open over the top half of him and again over the lower half of him. It was all one lid like a chest freezer, and I supposed that design gave the construction sturdiness so it wouldn't sag or fold in the middle.

I also learned from Twitch that Dad had not wanted to be embalmed so what service there was had to take place the following day after his death. I swallowed hard at this. This service would take place in less than twenty-four hours. *Where is he now? In the green room?*

"You going to be here a while? I need to take a walk." I left Twitch and Momma in our farmhouse kitchen.

Twitch nodded. He scraped a chair—not Dad's—across the floor and sat down by Momma. He placed his hand on her back and she leaned into him but was quiet.

*

I went outside. First, I entered the barn. The dogs had followed me there. They had often accompanied Dad in the barn. He talked to them and fed them summer sausage from his lunch pail.

It was summer. The barn was warm from the sun. The air was thick, stuffy. Dad's small wood stove stood idle and cold by his work bench. A series of birdhouses lined the surface of the work area. Dad had said, tongue in cheek, that like the other great painters he was having a period. He said he was in his yellow period which for him meant he painted his single design birdhouses various shades of yellow. Lemon to banana, school bus to taxi, cheese, corn, and yolk. He made yellows mixing this and that with the can of paint he'd bought with his discount at the lumber yard.

I peeked in the gray galvanized pail of water where he doused his finished cigarettes. Filterless butts floated on the surface of the water like grubs at the pool. Grains of tobacco drifted and bobbed along the plane of water like ineffectual life rafts. I kicked the bucket and then laughed at the irony as the putrid mixture spilled onto the barn floor. He was not there.

Next, I walked down our driveway, across the blacktop, and took the windy road toward the lake. I call it a road, but it was more a treeless incline that erosion had made. The exposed rocks were like acne jutting from the sand and clay. Trees swayed. Bugs churred and birds gossiped from the air and branches of oaks and maples. I was certain they talked about Dad having died and passed the word to the animals on the ground.

When our dock on Little Swan Lake came into view, I had expected he might be standing there holding his cane pole. He could take the rowboat, which was his preference, or fish from the dock, which was mine. I scanned the shoreline of grasses and swaying cattails, the lake, and the few neighboring cabins I could see. He wasn't there.

I didn't know where to place him. I couldn't imagine him playing a harp in the clouds or gorging himself at a banquet. Although, if a banquet had been the expectation, he would have eaten his fill of fish, chicken, and steak before he wasted stomach space on vegetables or desserts. Maybe he was at Fleet Farm. I'd check the aisle where they sold the chocolate covered peanuts or maybe the section where they had the hydraulic wood splitters.

I returned to the house not having any more answers than I had when I left. Momma and Twitch were still in the kitchen. I turned off my phone, went upstairs to my most recent assigned bedroom—not the downstairs one where I'd shared my first eighteen years with Becky. I couldn't go into that room any more than I could go into Momma and Dad's bedroom right then. Even though I looked for him I was still afraid of ghosts.

Chapter Twenty-Four

Celebration of Life

Funeral clothes pinch and chafe in order to give a person another more manageable pain sensation. That was the conclusion I reached as I sat on my bed examining my feelings about Dad. I don't think I knew all the things I felt about my dad until he was gone. I'm probably not unusual in that. I think kids reach a certain age where they stop idolizing even the parent they like and feel embarrassed by both of them. My heart was convicted, and I regretted every time I splashed him with my anger, greed, and my selfish disappointment. Like short, vivid movie clips memories flooded my mind looping and repeating. I was the fool in every scene. And he, Dad, was patient and long suffering. Had I killed him slowly with my drama and hardheaded ways?

*

The service was held at the Catholic Church because a Catholic priest who Dad used to drink with, when both men were younger, came to officiate. It wasn't at our church and it would not be Pastor Grind presiding over the service. If Grind's undies were in a bunch about it, he had the grace to not say anything. I was beginning to realize he, too, had more grace to him than I had recognized before.

Officiate is a loose translation of what happened that day. As people from Bend came in singly and in small groups and peered at Dad in the box, Father McQuire played guitar and sang patriotic songs he knew Dad would have appreciated. Dad had an outsized, sentimental adoration for the military even though his own stint with the army was short and may or may not have ended when, while drinking, he put his foot through a glass window and suffered a damaged Achilles.

The "Battle Hymn of the Republic," "America the Beautiful," and "God Bless America" would have choked him up and made his eyes water and nose run. I hoped if he were hearing those tunes he was completely healed and didn't dissolve into a coughing fit.

I didn't know all the things I felt for my dad until he was dead and I sure as hell didn't know what other people thought of him until the people started arriving at the impromptu celebration of his life. Like what was done for Chinese emperors, Egyptian pharaohs, and the poorest of nations people said their goodbyes to Dad and some people slipped tokens of appreciation in the coffin with him: a pack of filterless Camel cigarettes, a can of Grain Belt beer, two bottles of Grain Belt, a vacuum-packed stick of summer sausage, and a bottle of Corona beer. Dad said

Corona was actually the bottled urine of someone who drank a good beer. Some folks dropped in hats. Dad loved a free hat. I don't think he cared if it had a logo from a trucking company, seed corn brand, or a sports team. Free hats were valuable.

There were loads of cards accumulating in a wicker basket on the communion table. Later I would learn they were modestly stuffed with fives and single dollar bills which fit Dad. He wouldn't have gone for gaudy exhibitions of wealth. He made his own way and didn't want to be beholden to anyone and certainly wouldn't have wanted to take the food from someone else's table by expecting people to give what they couldn't afford.

I can't remember whether Father McGuire said anything about God or that we sang any hymns. The only scripture was a well-worn chunk from Ecclesiastes 3. I recognized the lines, "a time to be born and a time to die" but what stuck with me was verse eleven through fourteen:

"God has made everything beautiful in its own time. God has also set eternity in the human heart; yet no one can fathom what God has done from the beginning to end. I know that there is nothing better for people than to be happy and do good while they live. That each of them may eat and drink, and find satisfaction in all their toil—this is the gift of God. I know that everything God does will endure forever; nothing can be added to it and nothing taken from it."

Dad would have liked the mention of doing good and eating and drinking.

At one point, a woman I didn't know well but who knew Dad stood up and sang "The Rose." I later learned Dad had heard her sing the song before and told her how much he loved it. She belted out the ballad without benefit of accompaniment and I understood what he must have heard when she sang it. There was heart there, but no pretension.

I sat with Momma, Twitch, Kenny, and Ramona. Little Man, Allan was at the service. He ran freely back and forth between the pew where Kenny and Ramona sat and Dad's body in the box up front. I'm sure he was confused that his grandpa didn't wake up and take him into his arms—help him get outside where things were infinitely more interesting than in this big church with seated people staring forward at Grandpa sleeping and a stranger playing guitar and singing songs Allan had likely never heard before.

Ricky, Russ, Frankie, Justin, Charity, and Marin sat in the pew behind our family. I could feel their eyes on me. I suppose they wondered what I'd do. Would this be the impetus of my final crack-up or breakdown? I probably wondered the same thing.

At the funeral, the Becky in my head was strangely quiet, but not silent. She hummed snippets of the old-fashioned hymns I'd grown up with and heard at funerals: "Rock of Ages," "In the Garden," "Amazing Grace," and "Abide with Me." I suppose she was grieving too. I might have heard her hiss something about me out gallivanting around for queers' rights when I should have been at the hospital with our dying father. It was more of a whisper than anything. Again, there were no words. At the very end of the service, I noticed Mickey join Marin at the end of the pew. I smiled at her and she winked at me. I figured this to be Mickey-speak for, "You'll get through this, but stop by the lake for a tune-up just the same."

There were people at the service I didn't recognize. I suppose some of them could have been people new to Bend or people Dad had met in his work. Many of them had small rainbow pins on their shirts. I suspected some of the strangers were from the PFLAG group I heard Dad had attended. They paid their respect to my dad because he was one of their own—a parent who loved a child who not everybody agreed deserved love and support.

"Real sorry to hear of Joseph's passing. He was a spitfire at the PFLAG meeting," one man said to me as he shook my hand. He showed me a picture of his son Charles who was gay and living in the Metro area. Another man hugged me and said, "I hope you know how much your dad loved you. He was very proud of you and took some credit for your love of animals." I learned this man's daughter had gender dysphoria and didn't find her place or peace in the world before she took her own life at twenty-five.

A woman I didn't recognize took my hand. "You're part of the club of us who have lost a parent. It's hard, but you'll get through it. From what I could tell of your dad he's with you, loving you and watching over you every minute." She choked back tears, squeezed my hand, and walked away. I guess we were both reluctant members of the club she mentioned.

Several of the parents expressed their disappointment that they had not been able to ask the questions they'd come to ask Warren McGerber during the town hall meeting. "I suppose the important thing is that he has been arrested, but that meeting would have been a good place to open a discussion. You can bet you aren't the only queer in this town or district, Lorraine."

Many of the same people who made a point to talk with me also sought out Twitch. They hugged him or shook his hand. I heard one person call Momma Liz Taylor and they hugged Momma like they were long-lost friends who hadn't seen each other in years. They obviously didn't know the Momma I knew, or they wouldn't have laid hands on her uninvited. Still, Momma didn't slug, bite, or kick them. She received their touch with the passivity that to me made her look drugged or softened.

Later, I learned through another PFLAG member Momma attended a few online meetings with other parents and she used the screen name Liz Taylor without the worry that claiming the name of such a well-known Hollywood beauty would make people laugh at her stretch and bravado. Maybe she was being who she felt she was inside.

The funeral was endless and over too soon. When the realization hit me that they were going to take Dad's body, I felt panicky. I wouldn't ever see him again or I didn't know where to look. I talked to Gibson, one of the funeral home men, and told him to remove the various send-off offerings of beer before they put Dad's body in the crematorium chamber. Vomit rose in my throat as I said it. I couldn't bring myself to use the word oven. Somehow, I thought it important to protect Dad from glass fragments, but I couldn't stand thinking about the impending jet-engine column of flames.

My admonitions were likely wasted on the family who had performed this important community ritual for generations. They kindly listened, understanding there were few things in my control, and I was forced to trust they treated him respectfully.

I read the brochure. It takes two to three hours for the human body to burn to ashes depending on bone structure. I say ashes but he would be reduced to a few pounds of bone fragments and any remaining hardware from the cheap container. These were interesting details, and I would like to have talked with Dad about the practice generally, but it was grim, ghoulish, and unspeakable when the details are attached to someone I loved and someone who was kind, fished, and had a yellow period while painting birdhouses.

Chapter Twenty-Five

Home on the Farm

There was a luncheon in the church basement after the short service. It had long been a funeral rite in Bend for the community to eat goulash, white buns, and box cakes after a death. I don't remember eating anything. I think I heard Becky mention that she wasn't hungry either. I remember talking with people but none of the specific words that were said. Marin and Charity were there. I wanted them to whisk me away, but then again, I didn't know what I would say to the both of them. Eventually we migrated to the farm.

Kenny and Ramona took Allan back home to take a nap and check on Ramona's mom. Justin planned to leave for home later in the day. He and Frankie exchanged digits and maybe bodily fluids. I didn't know or care but was certain Frankie would tell me in her own time. Russ, Ricky, Frankie, and Justin stumbled around in our yard. I overheard Frankie get her daily call from her dad.

"You betcha, General. It's still with me." Frankie winked at me as she spoke on the phone with her dad. I envied her. "I love you, Dad. I'm with Lorraine. Her dad died last night. I know you love me too. Nothing changes that. I'll see you in a few days. Kiss Mom for me."

It was sweet having them all at the farm, but they didn't know what to do and I didn't know what to do with them. After Frankie ended her call, I put them out of their misery and told them to go home. It wasn't expected that they keep vigil over Momma and me. Twitch was there. Marin and Charity were there. After the others cleared out Momma and Twitch retreated to the kitchen. Momma put on a pot of coffee. Marin, Charity, and I sat in the living room. I purposely sat in an armchair. I didn't want to be sandwiched between them on the couch.

The silence was deafening. I resisted the temptation to fill in the space with patter. I felt like an empty Pez dispenser where at one time I couldn't keep from spitting out neat bits of information and opinion. I would never be charming again.

I thought I had a certain immunity since I played the role of the grieving daughter. Marin talked and moved first. Perhaps it was anxiety or her vocation as a social worker but she asked if I needed anything and checked in with Twitch and Momma. Were any of us hungry? We were not. She tidied. It wasn't that our house was messy. Neither Momma or I had been there much to mess it up and Dad—well, we all knew how he fit in this equation.

Marin filled the dogs' dishes with dry food and freshened their water bowls. She asked if there were other livestock that needed attention? There weren't. I assured her that all the beasts we had were fed, watered, and happy to sit and be numb.

My hint wasn't subtle enough. She asked Momma for permission to organize the countertops and refrigerator. Normally, Momma would have expressed profound offence, the implication being Momma had let the countertops and refrigerator become disorganized, but Momma allowed it. She and I hadn't been home so the offerings of meals to ease the suffering of people with sick ones had been delayed and morphed into "feed the grievers." The countertops were crowded with CorningWare and Tupperware, and reusable plastic containers that would exist long after any of us needed feeding or storage.

Bringing food to our house was like trying to impress a master chef with your ability to boil an egg. Momma was the best cook in the area and possibly the world. Although, it must be said that Momma had stopped cooking or even talking about cooking since Dad got sick. She had no appetite it appeared, but she was able to counsel Marin on separating the sheep and the goats. "Toss out anything that looks odd or from a box. Toss out anything from Gerry Narrows."

Gerry Narrows, our neighbor and the Bend librarian, was a dear friend of our family but couldn't cook worth shit. I don't know if Momma knew Gerry was Marin's aunt or if that knowledge would have quelled the insult. Momma accused Gerry of making roadkill helper, but it was probably just a box mix with dehydrated vegetables, preservatives, and other chemicals left over from manufacturing during the wars.

While Marin tidied, Charity joined me in the living room by my armchair. She sat on the floor and hugged my leg the same way she would have entangled my arm if we were sitting side by side. She leaned her head against my knee.

Marin must have stood in the doorway a while before I noticed her. "Sorry to interrupt," she said.

That's another phrase along with "be calm" and "I'm fine" that is usually useless and a complete and utter lie. It means just the opposite. The person is very satisfied and possibly proud, expecting a reward for having interrupted something awful and the interrupted should feel shame as having been found out for wearing the same underwear and socks two days in a row or liking Enya's music.

"You're hardly interrupting anything here. I'm being a bump on a log and Charity is…"

"Yeah, what is Charity doing?" Marin asked. She had her hands on her hips and for a moment reminded me of Momma.

Charity disentangled herself, looked at her watchless wrist, and said, "Wow, look at the time. I have to be going." She was out of the door before I had gotten my butt out of the armchair. Momma and Twitch had left the kitchen to the front porch.

Marin and I were alone in the living room of our farmhouse for perhaps the first time in our courtship. The mood was anything but romantic. It was tense. I wanted to say that I couldn't be in trouble. I was the grieving daughter. Read the program.

"Lorraine, I look at you two and I can't help but see you still love her. You are still in love with her." Marin sat on the couch across the room from me. She was only a few feet away in practical terms, but she was moving into space emotionally at the speed of light. "Don't you see it?"

My words caught in my throat. "Yes…"

She didn't let me finish. She got up and left.

I was stunned. She was already in her truck leaving the yard by the time I got outside. I ran alongside her truck. She closed the truck window and didn't stop to hear any more. She drove out of the yard.

I came back onto the open porch. Momma said, "That went well."

Chapter Twenty-Six

Suspended Animation

When grieving, nothing should be expected of you. Maybe that's why people keep bringing food. Grievers should not be allowed to handle heavy equipment, do math, or make any big life-changing decisions for obvious reasons. Maybe I knew this, but I think grief impairs memory.

The following days were a blur. I know Twitch sat with Momma every day. I know the three of us ate together whenever someone decided we were hungry. I think it was Twitch who attempted to establish a routine of sorts, but mainly I drifted along like the three of us were on inner tubes in a lazy river. We should be careful not to fall in the brackish water; there were no rapids, but there was also no end in sight.

Charity came every day. Mostly, she just sat with me. She didn't require me to talk or move. At some point Twitch had retrieved Dad's ashes and I showed her. She helped me open the heavy mil plastic bag inside the container. We were in my room away from Momma and Twitch.

Becky said, "I can't watch this." She was barely audible.

Charity watched me as I ran my hands through the ashes hoping to find a fragment of bone big enough to keep. There weren't any. It would have been ghoulish to have asked ahead of time for something to keep.

The grayish particles of Dad's cremains dusted my hands. I tasted the dust. It wasn't what I expected. Shouldn't it taste like some element of him? It was tasteless grit. He wasn't in the ashes either.

Chapter Twenty-Seven

Finding My Words

Charity and I were together a lot. We touched, but we didn't make out or make love. It didn't feel like either of us were dieting or squelching our sexual appetite. It was more like we didn't need that intimacy right then.

I needed to talk with Marin. She didn't answer my calls, but I found her leaving work one afternoon two days before I was supposed to return to vet school. We sat on a bench outside the County Social Services building.

"The other day you said it was obvious that I was still in love with Charity and you left before I could finish what I wanted to say. Please let me say it to you now."

Marin looked at me for what felt like a long time and she appeared like her breath was shallow, like she fumed. Then, she nodded and looked down at her hands folded in her lap, not at me.

"Charity and I, we've never been around each other without being lovers unless you count when we first met.

Even then we were thinking about being together. We have no practice at this."

"But you said it was over," Marin said.

"It was. I supposed it was in my head, but my body, my heart"—I didn't say it, but I thought it, *my hormones*—"haven't caught up yet. Before they could, Dad was sick, and she was back from Europe and you were both here."

"What are we doing, Lorraine?" A tear rolled down her cheek as she gazed at me.

"I thought of what you said at the hospital when I told you that I slept at Charity's place the night before and had told Charity about the voices I was hearing before I told you. You said, 'It's not like we're married.' But it's like for us we have to act like it, be in a hurry, stake our claim, make our stand." I hated quoting Marin to Marin, but I was about to do it again.

"That's another one of the hard parts of being in an unaccepted class of people. It has not been natural to date and practice, play the field, and get to know many, many people before becoming a committed couple. We only had the example of straight couples and the sanitized, virginal version at that. The model I grew up with said if you are having sex with someone you should be married or headed that direction. I ignored the exceptions and got on the train with the perceived majority.

"You're right. I'm still in love with Charity and I can't promise anyone that I'd ever embrace any other condition. I'm not helpless letting life just happen to me. I could make a choice to not act on my feelings and I've done a good job of it since I've been back. At the same time, I can't speed through my feelings. I can't just stop loving Charity. Maybe others can do that but it's going to take me more time. And I don't know whether I want to strengthen those muscles. I love being in love with Charity."

"Are you together now?" Marin asked.

"No. I haven't told her how I feel. I wanted to talk with you."

"That's a first," Marin said. "Sorry."

"That's okay. You should be pissed. I wasn't honest with myself when you and I got together. I was as honest as I could be. I wanted what I said to be true, but my body and heart has never totally caught up with my words and wishes."

"How do you know that isn't happening again and in a week or two you will think you should have stayed with me?" Marin asked.

I blew air out. "I don't know. I just know for today I'm doing what is true for my heart. Maybe, when and if I tell Charity I am still in love with her she will laugh or politely tell me that's nice but irrelevant. I don't think so. I think I am her heart and that she knows that now too."

"You said 'if.' Are you still deciding whether you're going to tell her you're still in love with her?" Marin asked.

I didn't answer. I hadn't misspoken when I said "if," but I truly didn't know what I was going to do and for that moment I was comfortable with that ambivalence. I was the grieving daughter. I didn't have to make any big life decisions right then.

"Lorraine Tyler, I'm not going to tell you to give me a call if it doesn't work out with Charity. I'm going to be royally pissed at you for a very long time and I'm going to question how I could have fallen in love with someone who is as foolish and stupid as you." She stood up. "And I'm still going to miss you. And you don't realize it yet, but you're going to miss me and someday you'll realize you made a big mistake not holding on to Marin England. I hope I'm not there to see it. I hope you sit with that mistake by yourself."

She got in her truck. She quickly wiped away some tears before she left the parking lot.

I sat on the bench for another hour looking into the light of the day.

Chapter Twenty-Eight

Us, Living and Dead, Plus Twitch
Equals Five

The last day of break I found Momma sitting with Twitch on our open front porch. Momma was wearing her nursing uniform which signaled she was ready to go back to work and others should follow suit. They both stared into the yard. Momma had her notebook out and jotted notes. For once I wasn't too concerned her doodles and declarations had anything to do with me. Her thoughts, beliefs, and wishes written or spoken would not change who I was.

Based on her frowns, grunts, and gesticulations I surmised she was writing in her notebook about our farmyard. Our yard had always been a sore spot for my momma. Dad had told her, "I don't fight you on nothing else, but the yard is mine."

Dad's dominion over the yard meant that it attracted junk and tasteless lawn ornaments like cat hair on black stretch pants. Dad's perceived dominion of the yard didn't keep Momma from making stipulations and occasionally enforcing said stipulations under the cover of darkness by removing the garden gnomes, plastic skunks, and fake deer and heaving them into the dumpster by the convenience store.

Charity and I had rescued a few of these pilfered baubles and put them back in the yard. We did it not because either of us thought the lawn litter was particularly beautiful but because its sudden reappearance riled up Momma. At the same time, she couldn't complain about its second coming without admitting culpability in the original rapture.

Momma and Twitch stared out at the yard. I scanned it, too, to know what they saw. A pair of pink flamingos—well, one pink flamingo; Momma ran over the other one with the station wagon—was perched in the ground next to squirrel tableaus. Fake ducks and geese stood in the squirty-shit-covered grass decorated by our real ducks and geese. A family of apple-cheeked, smiling gnomes—well, part of a family of gnomes. Momma had run over Papa Gnome too.

In recent years, Dad had been caught up in the rekindled Star Wars mania. Ceramic statues of Ewoks, Yoda, and Chewbacca spotted the yard. Momma forbade Dad to put Darth Vader on our property because of his resemblance to Satan; and Luke Skywalker was barred because he looked queer to Momma.

She said Dad could have Princess Leia behind the barn if she could have Han Solo in her bedroom; and she told him R2-D2 was only allowed if it was mounted on a lawn mower that actually cut grass.

"Hello," I said as I came out onto the porch and sat in the swinging loveseat where Becky had read her women's magazines. "What are we supposed to do now?"

Twitch said, "Peggy and I were just talking. These are strange times, but your momma and I would hope that you will finish your schooling."

I glanced at Momma and then back at Twitch. He added, "I can keep an eye on things here. Oh, in case you haven't heard, the County Attorney is going ahead with assault and kidnapping charges against Lewis and Petey. They may get a work release program. Yours and Ricky's letter had a lot to do with that possibility. They each got ten years of probation, and they have to provide restitution. You and Ricky get a side of beef every year from the two men."

"How are they supposed to do that?" I asked.

"If they get the work release program it will be to work a farm like the Hollister place, live in the house there on release days, work the land, raise some cattle and their own hay and grain."

"That farm was set up for pigs," I said like I cared.

"It is," Momma piped up. "That's why I'm thinking about letting them work this land too. How would you feel about that?"

Momma asked my opinion on something. I was immediately suspicious. "You've already done it, haven't you?"

Momma snuck a peek at Twitch and then peered at me. "No, well, I have mentioned it to the County Attorney, and I asked Twitch's lawyer to draw up some papers, but I wanted to get your thoughts. I want to keep working at the clinic. It would be nice if there was somebody to give this place some attention and generate some income."

I couldn't argue with her, not then or ever really. "It sounds like a good idea. You won't just sell it, will you?" I asked.

"No, Lorraine. This place was almost everything to your dad. I know he would want you to have it if you wanted it. He would want you to have it as his legacy." Then she was more herself again and said, "I run it now and don't get any ideas about kicking me out just yet."

Twitch and I both smiled. "Like anybody would dare cross you, Momma," I said.

"They'd have hell to pay," Twitch said. He took Momma's hand.

Maybe it should have chapped my ass to see Twitch take Momma's hand or that she had let him, but it didn't. It didn't make me doubt her love for my dad. Momma, like most everybody, had the capacity to love more than one person at a time. Maybe the capacity to love more than one person was the way I most took after her.

Momma, Dad, and Twitch, the three of them together had been first loves of sorts. Twitch met Momma first, but he also made a point of bringing Dad to meet her at the diner all those years ago. Dad had told me that he'd fallen in love with Momma at first sight and that he was completely gone once he'd heard her. He told me that on the day he asked me if I loved Charity.

He'd gone on to tell me that when he met Momma for the first time, he had told Twitch right then and there he planned to marry Momma. He told me just seeing and hearing her he planned to "marry her, slather her in love and attention, fatten and roll around in her arms, have a big house and babies just like her."

At the time I heard him express that sentiment I was very angry with Momma. She had just ratted me out to Pastor Grind and I had lost my scholarship. Dad's declaration of love and devotion to Momma made me want to puke.

My repulsion didn't stop him from telling his story. He said once he'd met Momma, he knew he wanted a big kitchen with kids just like Momma and he wanted to tumble over those children, feed them and her, and never be hungry again. I understood him better at age twenty than I had at seventeen.

I remember his exact words. "I didn't know her name or one speck about her, but I knew that I could imagine spending my entire life with her. I couldn't wait to tell her." I knew the feeling. It had happened to me in Bend library.

When Dad got all gooey at the diner the first time he'd met Momma, Twitch could have told him he had designs on Momma himself. He could have dampened Dad's excitement by admitting he'd already slept with her. Twitch didn't. Why didn't he?

Over the couple of years I'd known Twitch was my biological father I had thought he'd dodged a bullet by not pursuing his relationship with her, but maybe it was his version of a moment of grace. Once he knew my dad, his best friend, loved Momma, he stepped away. He made a choice despite whatever feelings he had. I wondered how he'd done that? Of course, he's my biological father so I probably have those capabilities in me too. Twitch gave me his biology and Dad raised me. I came from good stock.

I remembered having asked Twitch once why he wasn't married. He'd said, "The best ones are taken or too smart to take up with someone like me." Maybe what he hadn't said was that he still loved Momma but would never get between Momma and Dad.

"I don't know if I have any right to ask this and please don't swat me, but are you and Twitch together now, Momma?"

Momma spoke first, "We have known each other a long time. We know how to fight and get along better than a lot of folks and right now we both have big holes in our hearts like you do."

I imagined cartoons where the character, usually an unlucky cat, hits the wall leaving a hole shaped like them. I pictured each of us having a hole in our hearts that roughly matched Dad's outline, right next to a smaller hole shaped like Becky.

"If that came to be, would you have a problem with it?" Momma asked.

"Would it bother you, Lorraine?" Twitch added.

I had to grin at the irony of Momma and Twitch asking me for my approval of them loving each other. I wanted to say something about at least they were still heterosexual, but I didn't crack wise. "Dad once told me that nobody decides who we love. I guess it goes for you too. Of course, you'll need to extend the same courtesy to me and who I love."

Twitch smirked. Momma glared at me. She said, "I'm working at it, Lorraine. Goodness knows I don't want to be at odds with you. It's exhausting." She leaned toward me, tilted her head, and said softly, "You're my daughter. I love you. You doubt my love and I guess I fall short at making you a believer." She leaned back again so she was even with Twitch.

"Sometimes, I get after you, but wait until you have kids of your own. I hope you do. You'll learn that as a parent you want to protect them from the judgments and unkindness of the world and you're pretty powerless to do it. Your love isn't enough."

"Your love is enough for me, Momma," I said and immediately started crying. She did too.

"I'll deal with the rest of the world and fight the battles ahead of me, but I need to know you don't stop loving me because I go my own way. I need you for my home base." I swallowed hard; tears continued flooding my eyes and I didn't know if I felt as courageous as my words, but I could act as if I was brave. I'd done it before.

Her voice was weak and strangled by her heart in her throat. Momma said, "I will always love you, Lorraine.

I'll always worry for you, too, but don't expect me to stay quiet."

"Yeah, I know it's not possible," I said as I winked at Twitch. "I can handle your commentary. I just need to know you have my back even though I'm queer." I couldn't say it any more directly.

Momma raised her hand that was clasped in Twitch's hand. "We will always have your back. I promise." Twitch smiled and then kissed Momma's hand.

How long had I waited to hear those words or something similar? I wished Dad was there to hear it too. He would have checked Momma's forehead for a fever or called the snowplows to salt and sand in hell because certainly it had frozen over.

"Well, now we got the most important things settled, I have to get back to school and I have my own love life to sort out." I stood up to leave.

"What is happening there?" Twitch asked.

"Are you dating both those women?" Momma asked.

I frowned at the two of them and sighed. "It might be too soon for me to process this with the two of you, but I do appreciate you asking. Let's just say I need to finish school, take time to grieve and heal from what we've all lost; then, maybe I will know and be able to declare where my heart is."

"Well, the location of your heart and hormones is pretty obvious," Momma said. Then she raised her free hand, looked down, and shook her head. "Sorry, not my business. I'm sure you'll do what you think is best. Say hi to Charity, Marin, and your other friends from us."

I kissed them both and left the farm I'd known my whole life feeling like during the last hour or so it had been transported to another dimension, some place where patience and tolerance was added to water along with the fluoride. Momma said she loved me and she'd have my back even though I was queer. What was this world coming to? For once, Becky kept her trap shut.

Chapter Twenty-Nine

My Life Is Bigger Than That Jar

I stopped at Grind's to look for Charity. My heart was aflutter and then in pain when Mrs. Grind said she wasn't there.

"Where is she?" *Please don't tell me she is back with Kelly.*

"She left last night. She said something about a consignment painting she needed to complete quickly. I would have thought she'd told you."

I would have thought so too.

Mrs. Grind looked at me like I was the runt of the litter, but I wasn't. I wasn't the same whiney teen who watched my scholarship snatched from my grasp. I was someone who works for what I want and accepts the help of others. I could rise above any circumstance by just following what was already in me and by asking for help from my friends.

I waved goodbye and drove to Russ and Ricky's place to pick up Frankie. They were all in the yard when I pulled my truck up to the house. Allan ran to me.

"Momma Ramona made you some sugar cookies. Frankie gave them all breasts made from M&M's."

I took Allan into my arms and hugged him tightly. I waited for Becky's instructions. She softly said, "You should put Allan down so he can play. He's got good family to look after him."

I kissed Allan's neck and put him on the ground. "Thanks for the cookies." I hugged Ramona and nodded at Kenny.

Ricky and Russ embraced me. Russ's mom Ruth waved from her chair. Allan had gone over to sit on her knee.

"I have one more stop before we leave town," I said to Frankie. "You can come with me to therapy or I'll pick you up here on the way back.

"Therapy? Again? You're becoming a junkie, Lorraine," Frankie said. "I'll wait for you in the truck while you get your head shrunk again." She loaded more bags in the truck than she'd come with. I knew she'd tell me the story that went with the additional luggage. She pushed her backpack through the open window on the passenger side of my truck.

"I want to gas up the truck in town before we head back to school."

"Fine with me. I'm starving," Frankie said. She noticed the small jar of jelly beans on the seat. She snatched them up, opened them, and stuffed a handful in her mouth. "I love these. They're the good ones."

I started to tell her to stop eating my beans but I changed my mind. "Give me a couple," I said.

"Why do you have a small bunch of jelly beans in a jar anyway?" Frankie gave me the last few beans.

"It's my therapist. Each bean is a trauma in my life. You know—being rejected for being queer, Becky dying in front of me, that sort of thing. We're counting the things that have marked and changed me. It's a rough tally," I said.

"That's weird," Frankie said. She tossed the empty jar back on the truck seat.

"Why?"

"Where's your jar of heart-stopping good things? It's lopsided to only count the sad, disappointing things. What about meeting me? What about the experiences with Marin or Charity? What about Allan?" She wiggled her eyebrows. "What about orgasms?"

"Can we not talk about sex right now?"

"I'm just saying the good things in our lives mark us and change us too. Did you see how many LGBTQIA friends and allies showed up at the town hall? Your dad's funeral? You can't tell me that's not worth a few chocolates or something."

I drove slowly thinking about what Frankie had said. Instead of going directly to Mickey's place I drove into town. I stopped at the Munch and Pump, gassed up the truck, and made some purchases. While Frankie shopped, I emptied and rinsed the jar of pickles I'd bought. Once Frankie had her stash of convenience store meats and energy drinks I drove to Mickey's place.

I took my time meandering through the trail leading to Mickey's cabin.

"You didn't tell me she lives in the middle of the forest." Frankie said she thought the outdoors should be cleaner and have fewer bugs.

I wondered if I'd ever come this way again and knew I probably would. Mickey was sitting on her porch with Tumor when I arrived. It was like she'd been expecting me or maybe it was like living some place so beautiful like our farm, you have to just sit there quiet and bear witness.

"You can come with me, you know."

"Nope, I'm going to enjoy some alone time with my goodies. I'm going to eat all these snacks, too, in case you are wondering."

"Just keep your goodies covered." I took my bag from the convenience store and got out of the truck.

Mickey stood up from where she'd been seated on her deck.

"I have something for you," I called out.

"Oh, what could that be?" Mickey said.

"Stay where you are, I'll bring it to you."

She sat down again and waited for me on the porch of the cabin. Tumor rested at her feet. Mickey smiled when I held up an empty jar.

"This is from Famous Dave's Spicy Pickle slices. Have you tried them? The jar probably still smells of them." I sniffed it and immediately wished I used soap when I rinsed it at the gas station bathroom. "I got another bag of Jelly Bellies and some other goodies and I have the jar you gave me." I sat in the Adirondack chair next to her and slid a table over for my purpose. "Feel free to eat any of my visual aids. Frankie and I already ate my trauma beans." I placed the empty baby food jar she'd given me on the table. It was dwarfed by the pickle jar.

"I've been thinking about what you've taught me and listening to some of my other people, particularly Frankie. I decided I needed a bigger jar for my life. Pretend Frankie and I didn't eat the trauma history beans. Pretend they are still in this jar." I poured the pretend jelly beans from my jar of traumas into the bigger jar.

"My life is bigger than this tiny jar with so many beans in it. My life is more than the tallying of sad things. You once told me traumas mark and change a person. I believe you're right but Frankie and being with my family reminded me other things besides traumas mark and change a person. Like having a good dad."

I held up a box of Whoppers and another of Milk Duds. "I like these even more than jelly beans." I opened both boxes and put a Whopper and a Milk Dud in the pickle jar with the pretend jelly beans. "Those are for me having a good dad." I dropped in another Milk Dud. "That's for having the most infuriating momma but being loved and cared for just the same. Here's a handful for having Twitch in my life.

"I could put a whole box or two in the jar for the joys I've had knowing Little Man. Being his aunt has marked and changed me too. It has expanded my heart and I can imagine the honor and burden of being a parent."

Mickey smiled but didn't interrupt.

"I could add a case for my time with Marin and another two cases for knowing Charity. Hell, I could add several boxes for my time with Becky, living and dead." I rolled my eyes, looking above my head. "She didn't say anything to that."

Mickey popped a Milk Dud in her mouth and chewed.

"My point is that my life is bigger than my traumas because I have had so many people who have loved me and so many life experiences that are beautiful and sacred. Those things need to be counted in the mix. They mitigate the other things and give me hope that I can face anything that comes at me. And there's people and groups of strangers who want to be helpers and I need to learn how to ask them for their help. My dad figured that out and he asked for help at the town hall meeting.

"Last year, when Ricky was in danger, I went off by myself to try to find out and bring to justice the men who hurt him. Ricky and I both almost got killed in the process and my actions caused the death of Dr. Jacks. While I've been home, I tried to catch Warren McGerber confessing his crimes and as I waited in the field alone, I was soon surrounded by friends who didn't want me to do things all on my own.

"At the town hall meeting, Pastor Grind took a stand against hate. LGBTQIA and PFLAG groups arrived to support love over hate because Frankie and even my dad have been trying their hand at using community organizing. Ricky got his memory back and courageously told the sheriff what happened to him. All around me people are doing their best to rise up and stand for what is good and what is loving."

I poured all the rest of the candy I had into the jar. "Just today, my momma told me she loved me." I could have sworn I hadn't a tear left in my head, but my body had made a bunch more to run down my face onto my neck and shirt. "And Momma said she and Twitch have my back even though I'm queer." I blubbered for a good few minutes saying those words. Mickey just let me cry. She didn't even offer me anything to wipe the tears and snot. Maybe she knew better than me our tears are holy water and to witness them from others is to be baptized in grace.

"Those things, those good things mark and change me too. I must rise and show I am stronger for both the losses and wins. I am better able to be a sister, daughter, lover, maybe even counseling patient for having both. And to focus on only one type of experience is to neglect and miss out on all that is rich in being a person on God's earth." I wiped my eyes and nose on the inside of my T-shirt. "I don't mean to sound preachy."

Mickey stood up and hugged me where I sat. When she pulled back, I could see she was crying. "Lorraine, you are something. I was supposed to be helping you and you soaked up everything I knew to say and added another layer of good sense to it. You're going to be okay."

I swallowed hard and nodded my thick head. "I think I am. My heart is bruised missing Dad. I don't know where to find him."

"Maybe he will find you some way," she said.

"I kind of hope it isn't a voice in my head, but I suppose I'd take that too. He would tell me animal stories instead of criticizing me." I stood up. "Thanks for listening to me and helping me. I hope I can visit you again."

"You're always welcome." She gave me a quick hug and waved goodbye.

"I gotta say your head looks just as big as usual," Frankie chirped, licking her fingers to get every bit of grease from the convenience store cheddar dog. "Are you sure you've been properly therapized? And tell me about the dog. He has to be on his last four legs."

"Frankie, I challenge you to be quiet for ten minutes—five even. I want to just be quiet for a while. Help me, please."

She twisted and squirmed in her seat probably both insulted and daunted at the request. "Well, I can be quiet. I can be quiet for days if I needed to be."

I stopped the truck and glared at her.

"Fine." She mimicked having zipped her mouth closed. True to Frankie she added, "I'll just practice my sign language."

I noticed she started with the swear words she knew but at least it was quiet.

As I snaked through the windy driveway leading to Mickey's cabin the red fox appeared on my left. I put my hand on Frankie. "Stay quiet."

"If you just told me you were meeting up with a vixen, I would have understood."

"Shh, it's the male."

The fox stood by the side of the trail looking at me from a rise of dirt and rocks. His head was held high. He didn't look frightened of me, maybe curious. Then a vixen joined him there. She was smaller and looked at me more warily. Just as quickly as she had joined the male, two kits peeked their heads out from the grasses but didn't venture closer to me.

The pups were probably only two or three months old. By six months they would be hard to tell apart from adults. They would stay with their parents until they were seven months. By ten months, they'd be full grown. For right now, they were home-schooled.

I sat in my truck looking at the adult male fox mostly. He looked back at me. Like the rest of the world, I didn't know what the fox says. I could only watch. It may have been my imagination, but I could swear the male fox nodded at me. Then he turned and ran off into the woods, his partner and twins trailing behind him. I felt like I'd been given a present, but it was hard to explain. Dad would get it. Twitch would understand.

Surprisingly, so did Becky. "He's going to be okay, isn't he, Lorraine? Little Man is okay. You're okay—well, as good as you'd expect. Everybody is okay."

"Yeah, we're all going to be okay," I said out loud.

"You know, Lorraine, I think you're right," Frankie said. "Can I talk again? I can be quiet if I need to, but I've truly never needed to. May I speak freely?"

"Go ahead, I'm listening."

"Finally, I can tell you all about my time with Justin," Frankie said. Just as she began her dad called. "Dad, I'm on my way home with all my parts." Frankie glanced at me. I expected she would hang up, but she didn't. "Dad, I love you and Mom too much to leave you out of my life. I want you to know I scheduled my surgery. I have most of the money I need, of course I'll have to quit vet school for a while if I use up my savings. It's okay. I can work, save, and take out loans. Please don't interrupt. I know this is a lot to take in, but I hope you know I was raised right, and I know what I'm doing. Oh, and Lorraine is going to help me start an LGBTQIA rights group in town. Aren't you, Lorraine?"

"Yes, I am," I said a little loudly like I wanted Frankie's parents to hear my pledge.

"I'll call you when I get home. Oh, one more thing, I want to tell you about a boy I met." Frankie hung up her phone and turned it off. "That should spark some lively conversation at headquarters. Where was I?"

"You were telling me about Justin," I said.

"Yes of course, Justin. Don't you love his name? It's the name of a superhero. Can't you just picture him in a cape and tights? Have you ever seen a more handsome man?"

None of these questions were meant for me to answer. They were in fact Frankie's statements of her truth. I just listened. She would answer any questions I had in her own time and Frankie-esque way.

"Well, I kept him off balance. Mystery is very romantic. I didn't apologize or explain anything for one maybe two whole days. I just flirted and let him get to know me and naturally fall in love on his own. Which, of course, he did. I didn't touch him. It was hard, Lorraine." She took my arm but not enough to impede my steering. "I wanted to kiss him from the moment I saw him. I wanted to run my hands over his muscled neck, shoulders, and chest. It's lucky that his face is so beautiful to stare at and distracting or I might have lost complete control." She shook her head side to side, lost in the memory.

I grew impatient with Frankie's narrative style. "Did you ever kiss him?" I asked. I hoped to get away from the body parts description.

"Yes, we kissed, but nothing more. No making out, no petting, no groping, no dry..."

"I get the idea, Frankie."

"I told him I wasn't that kind of girl." She giggled. "Of course, he can tell I'm just that kind of girl, but he didn't laugh at me. He didn't push me or taunt me. It was like we were agreeing to wait to have sex until we were married. We won't, but we did this week."

"Wow, I must say I'm surprised, Frankie. I thought you would be all over each other."

"I know, so did I. I can't really explain it. My therapist has me reading these articles about transitioning from the perspective of those who have done it and other people in their life. Some people expect to finally be happy when they get the body alignment they want, and some are and some are not. One researcher likened the surgical aspect of transitioning to treating a wound." Frankie looked out of the passenger window for a while before she spoke again.

"Justin was really into me without sex or seeing what my private junk looks like now or hearing about what I plan to do. It was nice just kissing and flirting. Besides, you and I have vet school to finish and money to save. Who would counsel you on your love life, if I was all involved with that perfect specimen of manhood? Sex with him possibly depletes brain cells." She sighed heavily. "I'm tired now. Wake me when we get home."

Frankie nested on her side of the truck and fell asleep before we were out of the county. I bet she dreamed of Justin or convenience store food. I let her sleep and enjoyed the quiet of the ride.

When I was nearer to Duluth the big lake came into view and in some ways, I felt like I was seeing it for the first time. The waters splashed and battered its basalt shoreline. I'd always felt more comfortable with the more manageable sized lakes of Central Minnesota. Before it was like I feared Lake Superior was so big and unpredictable it could reach out and grab me if I didn't keep watch.

Lake Superior, or one of the Ojibwa names, gichi-gami, lived up to its name in every way. It was the largest freshwater lake in the world by surface area, roughly the size of South Carolina. If someone drained it, its waters would cover North and South America. It both awed me and scared the crap out of me that it could cover and swallow up anything and everything in the world I'd ever loved, but that day, the drive to the lake was just something else both dangerous and beautiful. It had no designs on hurting me. It had no dominance over me unless I chose to throw myself into its powerful surf. I smiled to myself.

When Frankie and I got to our apartment complex, I noticed Charity's truck parked in the lot.

"I hope you don't mind that I gave Charity my keys. She's in town doing a commissioned work," Frankie said.

I didn't think much about this as we jabbered with each other and lugged Frankie's bags to the apartment. Frankie was hungry again and already talking about what to order out or where to go for dinner.

I heard music from a pop radio station as I got closer to our door. The apartment door was unlocked. I found Charity barefooted, dressed in shorts and a T-shirt. She was dotted and smudged with paint.

"What on earth?" I dropped Frankie's bag where I stood and just stared. The large wall of the living room sported the outline of a new mural, a scene I'd recognize anywhere. A picture I carried in my heart alongside my family and friends.

"You did this?" I said like I'd been cast as Captain Obvious instead of the grieving daughter.

It was Bend, Minnesota, an aerial view I guess you'd call it. The locales were not detailed, more like suggested, but I saw everything I cared about. Our farm was west of town next to Gerry Narrows's farm and the Hollister place. I could see the school, Natvig football field, the baseball and softball diamonds. Two rows of businesses smiling like straight teeth. Twitch's vet office was in the middle of the block just down from the grocery store and kitty-corner from the Bend Clinic where Momma worked.

The churches in Bend were more like molars, in the back behind the front row. I could see them there making everything that came Bend's way sometimes bigger than it needed to be and sometimes smaller and easier to swallow.

It wasn't prominent but I saw the place along the county line where Ricky was attacked and where later Warren McGerber stung Lewis and I instead of vice versa. That was a setting of trauma, but it was also a place where I found out I had a posse of friends who didn't expect me to do everything on my own.

There were lakes of course. I spied Little Swan Lake right away. I imagined where Mickey's cabin sat and where our dock sheltered small pan fish in the shallows. The fox family lived in those woods. The land held the bodies of those who had died. Native Americans had dropped their arrowheads and lost their land and lives in the hills and plains of that country.

"What made you think of doing this?" I put my arm around Charity.

She turned and put her arm around my shoulder so we could both look at the painting but be touching. "You always miss Bend when you are away. I hoped being able to see this depiction of it every day would make it easier to finish school. Besides, the best of Bend goes wherever you do."

I thought about telling her she was part of my idea of the best of Bend, but I also knew it had been my dream to live in Bend...not Charity's. I didn't tell her I was still in love with her and I had been since the first day we had met. It wasn't any less true but not every thought or feeling had to be blurted out in the world. Feelings come and go. Each of us has to think about how we feel and make a decision on what we will do. My nerves were raw, exposed. It wasn't the time to worry about my love life.

No matter what came my way, trauma or blessing I would examine how it had marked and changed me. Maybe I'd put it in a jar. Maybe I'd keep a tally but wouldn't just count the hard things. I'd count the blessings and wonders too. They count. They mark and change me.

I kissed Charity's cheek. "Thank you, Charity. This was very thoughtful. I love it." Then I stood on my own.

Frankie sniffed, "Aww, I think I'm going to cry. Do you need me to leave while you two have a moment? I probably have something I could go shave or moisturize."

"You're fine, Frankie," I said. "Charity and I are two people who love each other. Love doesn't end. Now, we're two people talking. We have room for you."

"You're going to be a vet, Raine," Charity said.

"Yep. You're an artist," I said.

"Yep." Charity folded her arms on her chest and stared forward at her painting.

"We can still love each other and be who we were meant to be, and we don't have to decide what that looks like right now," I said.

"Let's see where our passions take us," Frankie said as she wiped tears from her eyes.

Out of the corner of my eye I spied Charity nodding.

That was a good sign.

Acknowledgements

Thank you, Raevyn McCann and NineStar Press for publishing *Rise*. Thank you, Elizabeth Coldwell (there may be more editors to include here) for helping make *Rise* a better book. Any time I have missed the mark and gave my characters language or actions that hurt others it is my authorial decision and not the fault of editors. My editors have painstakingly combed this manuscript for transphobic and fat shaming language. Where anything still reads like that it was my decision to allow my characters to be imperfect and still learning how language, even in jest, affects feelings and perceptions. No malice is intended.

Thank you, Natasha Snow for another stunning cover.

Thanks to Sharon Belcastro and Ella Marie Shupe from the Belcastro Agency for championing my work and finding a place for it in the publishing world.

Special thanks to my cousin Irene Allord, who connected me with Kathy Solem and the Buffalo Gals' book club. My first book, *Bend*, was so real to them that they had a very spirited discussion about the paternity of my characters. Their speculations inspired part of the plot of *Rise*. Additionally, they are a really fun group of people.

Thank you to all the book groups, breweries, libraries, and bookstores that have allowed me to visit, sell my book and read. COVID curbed these opportunities this past year but it makes me even more grateful for the opportunities I have had since my first book came out. Thank you, readers. You have given your precious time to read my books. I am honored.

About Nancy J. Hedin

Nancy Hedin, a Minnesota writer, has been a pastor and bartender (at the same time). She has been a stand-up comic and a mental health crisis worker (at the same time). She wants readers to know that every story she writes begins with her hearing voices.

In 2018 Nancy's debut novel, *Bend*, was named one of twenty-five books to read for Pride Month Barnes and Noble and was named Debut Novel of the Year by Golden Crown Literary Society and Foreword Indies Honorable Mention for GLBT Adult Novel of the Year. Her second novel, *Stray*, was a finalist for the Minnesota Book Award in Novel and Short Stories.

Email
njhedin@yahoo.com

Facebook
www.facebook.com/nancy.hedin.3

Twitter
@njhedin1

Website
www.nancyhedin.com

Other NineStar books by this author

Stray

Also from NineStar Press

Liquid Courage by Stephanie Shea

Alexandria Van Kirk has always been a slave to her romantic nature. When a night of liquid courage lands her in bed with one of her best friends, Alex is confronted by a host of feelings that terrify her. Feelings about her friend and, unexpectedly, a barista from her favorite café.

It's a tug of war between heart and body. Desire against all her daydreams of someone to share silence, sunsets, and coffee with.

But Alex's past is also about to catch up with her. Tortured memories and the girl they're all about. It's like fighting the pull of a whirlwind. A surefire losing battle. But embracing a newfound romance amid the return of an old flame is a precarious balance, one not even Alex herself is sure she can manage.

How the hell does she choose between the girl she loves and the one she could never confess loving to begin with?

Love in the Shadows by Maggie Doolin

Meg Mitchell is about to enter her final year of secondary school in the small close-knit village of Tullybawn in rural Ireland. But even at eighteen, she has never had the joyful experience of first love with any of the boys she has met or gone out with.

However, that's about to change with the arrival of dynamic young English teacher, Harriet Smith. Under the charismatic Harriet, Meg blossoms and discovers that she has a real talent for English. She also finds herself inexplicably drawn to Harriet.

Over time, Meg's feelings deepen, but this is 1970s Ireland where homosexuality is still a crime, where sex of any description is never discussed, and where an all–powerful harsh and repressive Catholic Church holds sway over every aspect of family life.

In this climate, Meg will face many challenges, from her family, her community, and her own desires. She will have to choose a path forward despite difficulties that, at times, seem insurmountable.

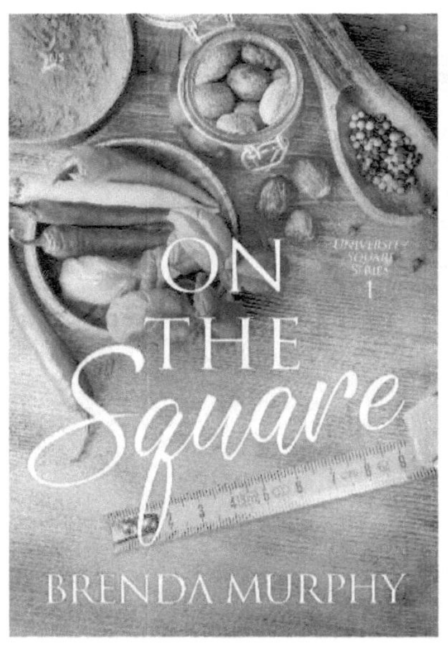

On the Square by Brenda Murphy

Dropped from her television show after a very public split with her cheating ex, celebrity chef Mai Li wants nothing more than to reopen her parents' shuttered restaurant and make a fresh start in her former hometown. So what if twenty years of neglect has left the building in need of a major renovation?

Seduced by Mai's charm and determination, hard-edged contractor Dale Miller agrees to take on her renovation project.

After a spring storm causes significant damage to the building and renovation costs exceed Mai's budget, Dale offers her a deal, but is it a price Mai is willing to pay?

Connect with NineStar Press

www.ninestarpress.com

www.facebook.com/ninestarpress

www.facebook.com/groups/NineStarNiche

www.twitter.com/ninestarpress

www.instagram.com/ninestarpress